ROMANTIC SHORT STORIES

Harlequin Books

TORONTO • NEW YORK • LONDON • PARIS • AMSTERDAM
STOCKHOLM • HAMBURG • ATHENS • MILAN • TOKYO • SYDNEY

HARLEQUIN'S ROMANTIC SHORT STORIES

The publisher acknowledges the copyright holders of the component stories
as follows:

Once Upon a Time
Copyright © 1979 by Greta Nelson

Return to Eden
Copyright © 1979 by Elizabeth Case

The Smile on the Face of Miss Pringle
Copyright © 1979 by Roma Grover

When Winter Comes
Copyright © 1977 by Maureen Lee

Farmer Jo
Copyright © 1978 by Frances Melvin

The Commission
Copyright © 1975 by Rachel Murray

Life is for Living
Copyright © 1984 by Jo Francis

Waiting for Grizelda
Copyright © 1978 by Roma Grover

Fathers' Race
Copyright © 1983 by Gemma Leighton

Beginnings
Copyright ©1977 by Greta Nelson

Cover illustration by P. Gonzalez
Story illustrations by Shirley M. Clemmer

ISBN 0-373-82450-5   ISBN 0-373-82450-COMP

CONTENTS

1 | ONCE UPON A TIME
BY GRETA NELSON

Jon Markham approached his romantic dalliances with all the planning and strategy of a military maneuver.

He left nothing to chance, and this evening was no exception. He'd borrowed his sister's apartment (Maggie having considerately taken a week's early holiday), and he'd spent the afternoon preparing his rather special exclusive-to-him paella. The wine was cooling, the lights were suitably dimmed, and he had taken a great deal of care in selecting the dreamy, romantic music already poised on the record player.

In short, his campaign plan was coming along nicely. He took time off to have a quick drink and recognized within himself that wave of feeling that was becoming too familiar. Boredom? Depression? A sense of wondering if it was all worth the effort?

He supposed the pattern was now just too well-worn. He saw his quarry, liked it, stalked it, and depending on the circumstances, became entangled or not. Mostly the latter. In his job as a fashion photographer he spent his entire life among the most incredibly beautiful women. Some appealed, some were harder to woo than others, but nowhere, as yet, had he met anyone who had ever begun to inspire a solemn commitment, a do-or-die awareness that this was it.

And Jon found it all vaguely disturbing, because, truth to tell, despite his voguish approach to life, deep down within him there lurked a romantic.

Jon downed his drink *and*, he hoped, his irritation at his present line of thought. It was becoming too frequent, too insidious, this perpetual self-analysis, this inability to enjoy what life offered.

Tonight the lovely Francesca was swimming into his net. Francesca was the latest golden girl in the rapid turnover of top cover girls. She was, Jon supposed, quite stunning. She was superb in front of the cameras, with white, even teeth, a perpetual suntan and long, long legs that seemed to go on forever. He'd made his play carefully and as subtly as he knew how, and yesterday she'd said yes to a dinner date tonight.

But after five minutes of euphoric satisfaction at his success, Jon had felt his triumph strangely diminish, so he had plunged into tonight's campaign plan and with even more determination than usual.

He glanced at his watch. Ten minutes to zero. He checked the paella, which was simmering with aromatic promise, and glanced at the table, attractively set for two. Then the doorbell shrilled, and Jon raised his eyebrows. She was early by ten minutes. Always a good sign.

His smile of welcome faded instantly, however, as he

opened the door. The girl in the hall was about five foot two, with spiky brown hair framing a face that was as pallid as skim milk. Her eyes were enormous in the white wedge of face and were fixed on Jon's in what he could only term desperation.

"Maggie?" she said, her voice sounding as though it was coming from way off. "Isn't this Maggie Markham's apartment?" And then she fainted, falling against him, so that he caught her before she hit the ground.

She was as light as a child, fragile and small boned, as if she could be crushed by the merest breath of wind.

Her head had fallen against his shoulder, her profile visible, and he looked down at the creamy skin, the pert, upturned nose, the sweet line of mouth, the long dark lashes feathering her cheeks.

Some almost forgotten recognition stirred in Jon, and he went on gazing into the still face.

And into this charmingly domestic scene stepped Francesca. The perfect mouth emitted a tight smile and she said, "Oh, dear, you double booked."

But she was really quite helpful in settling the girl into one of Maggie's single beds, and she telephoned for a doctor while Jon sponged the perspiration-soaked forehead, lifting the bangs that were as soft and brown as a bird's wing.

He turned to see Francesca watching him from the doorway.

"You're quite the Florence Nightingale," she said. "Who is she?"

Jon stood up and went to join Francesca in the lounge. "I'm not sure," he said, frowning. "She asked for Maggie, so she's obviously a friend of my sister's."

He raised his shoulders in protest. "I'm desperately sorry about all this."

He observed Francesca's marvelous hair, profuse and corn colored, and the beautifully cut cream skirt and blouse. He sighed at the waste of it all. "You look wonderful. And the evening will be just perfect once we've dealt with our little friend in there."

Francesca's smile was tepid, but she went to sit patiently on the settee while Jon paced between the paella and the bedroom.

The girl was sitting up when Jon slipped in for the fourth time. Her eyes looked bigger than ever, dark brown with flecks of amber, and there was defiance in them, courage alongside the wariness, and Jon Markham liked that.

He sat on the bed and smiled. (Not his spreading-the-net smile, but the one he used for his family and stray dogs and Tom-and-Jerry cartoons.)

"Well, here's a to-do," he said, sounding vaguely like something out of Dickens.

Tricia Harriott wondered how long she could manage to sit up without fainting again, but found the effort too much, so she allowed her head to sink back on the comfortable pillow and made a gigantic effort to speak.

"Look, I'm Tricia Harriott, and you are Jon. You obviously don't even remember me. I was at school with Maggie and I came to stay with you once." She attempted a smile for a brief moment and then sighed. "I've traveled down from Scotland, but I was stupid enough not to book a hotel in advance, and they are all crammed with visitors. Some sort of exhibition. Not a bed to be had. Then I thought about Maggie, but I didn't realize just how ghastly I was feeling. I walked from the station, thinking the fresh air would do me good. But it didn't...."

Jon saw the pallor take over again, spreading over her face so that every vestige of color drained away. He put the wet cloth on her forehead and was just about to call the doctor again when that worthy man arrived.

Jon plied Francesca with martinis and apologies while they awaited the diagnosis. It was an extraordinary situation. Here he was, with his plans crumbling to dust around him, and yet he felt no great devastation, no real disappointment. He was, in truth, extremely concerned about the Harriott girl, who looked like a waif and stray from some fairy tale.

Tricia Harriott. He sat up, as the elusive memories flooded back. Of course! Maggie's little school friend who had stayed with them years ago. She'd been about fourteen and had looked younger, and Jon had had to kiss her at the party during some fatuous game like forfeits. And he, feeling terribly grand and a bit of a roué at seventeen, had kissed her full on the mouth. Everyone had laughed, apart from the girl herself, who had looked at him with enormous, reproachful eyes.

Jon surfaced again to see that Francesca's glass was empty and that her immaculate nails were tapping a staccato rhythm on it. So he hastily got her another drink and was then summoned into the bedroom.

The doctor was cheerful and matter-of-fact.

"She has a rather nasty strain of flu. She's actually over the worst now, I imagine." He looked down at his patient. Her lashes were feathering her cheeks again and her mouth was looking a little nearer to tears. The doctor drew Jon outside.

"I really don't know how she managed to get here at all in that state. She's completely exhausted. Is she your girl friend?" His gaze lighted on Francesca on the settee. He looked back to Jon with a kind of reverential respect. "You chaps do seem to keep yourselves busy. But to get back to our patient, it really would be best if she could stay here for a couple of days. I'll pop in again tomorrow, but she must stay in bed."

His glance flickered to Francesca, then back to Jon. "She'll need plenty of hot liquids, and keep her warm. A couple of days should see her on the mend." He wrote out a prescription, waved a hand uncertainly at Francesca, and left.

It was definitely not one of his more successful evenings, Jon decided. By the time he'd nipped out to collect the prescription and give the first dose to the very sleepy, flushed-looking Tricia, the paella had somewhat given up the ghost. Which could also be said of Francesca, who toyed with her food and answered Jon's questions with a monosyllabic lack of enthusiasm. Not that Jon felt like talking much, anyway. It was decidedly cramping making overtures to Francesca, knowing that the prostrate Tricia was just beyond the bedroom door.

He gave up after a while, switched off the music, turned up the lights and halfheartedly arranged to repeat the evening on Saturday. He saw Francesca down to the parking lot, waved her off and went back to make an onslaught on the dishes.

And there, above the scrape of crockery and cutlery, he heard the unmistakable noise of female sobbing. Nothing dramatic, merely a subdued, suppressed sound, as though she was crying into her pillow.

Which was exactly what she was doing. Jon prodded her gently with his finger, and she turned over, looking up at him, her eyes luminous in the darkened room.

"Come on!" he said, sitting on the side of the bed. "It isn't as bad as all that. You've had some medicine, and the doctor says you'll be fighting fit the day after tomorrow."

He saw her lovely mouth pucker, as she shook her head in denial. "It's not that! I feel such a fool, butting into your evening and driving your beautiful friend away so early. You're not telling me that your sessions usually end as early as this—only when moronic females faint all over your doorstep and then play gooseberry for two days."

There was silence and Jon Markham was aware of a most extraordinary feeling, warm and tender, like shared laughter or childhood promises made and kept. It was the solid stuff of commitment and caring, and it warmed him so much that suddenly the next two days stretched ahead like a glorious, untapped adventure.

He looked at her elfin face, and his eyes lingered on her beautiful mouth. There would be no need of planned military maneuvers with this girl. There would be no need to impress. There would be fun and laughter and the die-hard standards that had formed his childhood and upbringing. He found it all marvelously exciting.

"I feel that we both need a strong cup of tea," he said. "Then masses of sleep for you. I'll phone your parents in the morning." He hesitated. "There's no one special I should be calling?"

Tricia smiled, her first real smile of the evening, and shook her head. "No one at all."

The moonlight had crept into the room, and her eyes were as brilliant as stars. Jon smiled down at her.

"I do remember you, Tricia Harriott," he said quietly. "In fact, I wonder if I ever really forgot you." And he bent down and kissed her, briefly, gently, undemandingly.

In the kitchen he boiled the kettle, made the tea and reflected happily on the never-ending magic of things.

2 | RETURN TO EDEN
BY ELIZABETH CASE

The turning down to Edenbrae looked much as I remembered it. There was one difference, though.

My grandfather would never have a sign put up with the name on it. He said that everybody knew where the Howies lived and anybody who didn't had only to ask. Now there was a signpost that said, To Edenbrae, and under it, Bed and Breakfast.

It was an excuse to go and look at the place again. Not that I really needed one. The approach road was a good half mile long, dipping its way between hedges and grassy banks, but the car covered the distance quickly. Much more quickly than the legs of a child, particularly with wild flowers to pick and birds flitting in and out of the hedgerows.

I stopped the car at the gate and sat and looked at the house for a long time. It was the same and yet it was different. The walls had been painted, the roof recently repaired; there were tubs of geraniums set around the paved yard. It had been swept clean in my grandmother's day, but never like this, as if no muddy boot had ever set foot on it. And where were the sounds and smells of the farmyard?

There was a painted sign on the gate, just as there had been at the end of the road. I smiled at the thought of what my boss would say if he saw where I was proposing to spend my hard-won holiday.

As usual he had thought up all sorts of excuses to postpone it.

"All the arrangements are made," I said firmly, "and I'm taking at least three weeks."

He protested that he couldn't possibly do without me all that time. I told him I had arranged for a temporary replacement. He looked cunning and said that no one was indispensable. I agreed with him. He had to give in then, because he knew I could walk into another secretarial post anywhere in the city.

"I suppose you're off to some glamorous place to bask in the tropical sun," he said mournfully.

"Something like that," I said.

And now here I was in southwest Scotland, in the middle of the lovely Galloway countryside, about to avail myself of an offer of bed and breakfast. I wound down the window and breathed deeply of the soft, clean air. Oh, it was good to be away from London, away from crowds and rush and fatigue.

I got out, opened the gate and from habit went around the side to the back door. The front door of a farmhouse is for ornament only. No dog barked, nor were there any multi-colored cats gliding around corners. I knocked on the back door. There was no reply so I knocked again.

"Come on in!" It was a woman's voice calling from somewhere above.

I pushed the door open and stopped in surprise at the sight of the functional modern kitchen. Gone was my grandmother's kitchen range that she had insisted on keeping, in spite of the family's persuasion. I could see that range now, black and gleaming steel at the edges, smell the soup simmering and the bread baking. Gone was the stone sink by the window with its one brass tap reflecting the sunlight, and the wooden table scrubbed to a whiteness that hurt your eyes. Now all was plastic and stainless steel.

"I'm up here," called the voice again. "Be with you in a minute."

Grandpa was twenty-five years older than grandma. He had gone to sea in his youth and gained his master's ticket before he retired at the age of forty-nine and came back to the place where he was born. Grandma was the daughter of one of his old friends, and when they met they fell madly in love.

She was the bonniest girl in all the world, grandpa said, and he knew what he was talking about. Everybody thought the age difference was too great, but they went ahead and got married and stayed in love for the rest of their lives. I remember still the little secret smile they would exchange when their eyes met. Being Scots, they made no outward demonstrations of love, but often they seemed to be shut away in a private world that held only the two of them....

There was a clatter of feet on the stairs, and the kitchen door flew open. A young woman stood there. Her tattered jeans and shirt were daubed with paint, and she had a smear of blue on her nose.

"Hello, who are you?" she asked, her gaze traveling

slowly from my fashionable hairdo to my expensive shoes.

I felt ridiculously overdressed. "I'm sorry if I surprised you," I said, "but you did call to me to come in. Could I have bed and breakfast, do you think?"

"Why, yes. I do have a vacancy, as it happens. Just for the one night?"

"I did think of staying for a week, perhaps longer, but of course if you're full, I'll quite understand...."

She laughed. "As a matter of fact, you're my very first guest. The sign only went up this morning, and then I decided the bathroom could do with a coat of paint. You're welcome to stay as long as you like. If you don't mind being practiced on, that is."

"Sounds great," I said, laughing with her. "I'm Alison Howie, by the way."

"And I'm Jill Hamilton. Perhaps you'd like to see your room."

She took me up the narrow stairway I remembered so well and showed me into the very room I had had as a child. The wardrobe and dressing table were modern, but the bed was the one with the brass rails and the round gleaming knob on each corner. I exclaimed in pleasure.

"It is a nice room isn't it?" said my landlady. "The view is terrific."

The view was as it had always been, out over the river to the hills where the dark green of the leafy trees crowded up to the skyline.

"I used to come here every summer," I said. "My grandfather had the farm then. And this was my room."

"When you were a child? How marvelous that you've come back! Let's bring in your case, shall we? And then we'll have a cup of tea and talk."

We had our tea in the kitchen, and I told her all about my grandparents and my holidays at the farm. Jill, as she told me to call her, had only lived there for a few years but she had heard of the Howies in connection with the house. It hadn't been a farm for quite some time. The land was taken over by another farmer, a Mr. Martin. Perhaps I'd heard of him because the family had been here from way back.

"And speak of the devil!" she said, looking out of the window. "Here comes one of them now."

The door opened and a man came in, ducking his head slightly as if he was used to lintels being a little too low. He was broad-shouldered to match and had straight, thick, dark hair and warm brown eyes. There was an incongruous dimple in his chin.

"Hello, Jill," he said. "Just came to see if there was any word from Andrew and young Philip."

He stopped when he saw me.

"This is one of the Martins I was telling you about. Ross Martin, Alison Howie."

"Ross!" I said. "I'd have known that dimple anywhere!"

"Alison! Alison Howie!"

We stood and grinned at each other like a couple of kids.

"Hey!" said Jill. "What's all this?"

And then we were shaking hands, and Ross was patting the top of my head, which is five feet eight inches from the ground, and telling me I hadn't grown much. Then we turned to Jill and explained that as children we had played together all summer, that we—Ross and Graeme, his older brother, and I—had been inseparable.

"How is Graeme?" I asked, perhaps too casually.

"Oh, he's fine. He runs the farm now, you know. Dad retired a few years ago."

"And you?"

"I'm a teacher, along with Jill's husband, at the comprehensive in the town. He's in Switzerland at the moment with a party of boys from the school."

"And I haven't heard from him yet. Nor from our son, Philip. If I know them they'll arrive home saying cheerfully, 'Didn't you get our postcard?'"

We all laughed.

"Are you married?" I asked Ross.

"No," he said. "And neither is Graeme."

Had he guessed that was what I really wanted to know?

"And yourself? I gather not when the name's still Howie. But why not?"

"Concentrating on my career. Or perhaps it's because nobody asked me."

"That I don't believe."

We sat and talked for the rest of the afternoon, interrupting each other to tell Jill of our childhood exploits, exchanging news of our families, but not saying much about our present-day lives. There was, after all, plenty of time.

Ross insisted that I come back with him to the farm for tea. This, I recollected, would be a hearty sit-down meal and not an affair of sandwiches and cups balanced in the hand. His mother and father, he said, had gone to Canada on a visit, but he and Graeme had a housekeeper, who would not be at all put out by the advent of an unexpected guest. It would be a grand surprise for Graeme.

I was not averse to surprising Graeme.

The Martin house looked prosperous. Graeme was there when we went in, and he was all I remembered. Even as a boy he had been handsome, but now his good looks were almost spectacular. There was a deftness, a sureness about him that Ross lacked, a decisiveness that would always get him what he wanted. He was genuinely pleased to see me, and I reveled in the admiration I saw in his eyes.

It was heady stuff being admired for myself and not just because I had a boss who was useful for an ambitious young man to know. It was a recent experience of that kind that had made me decide to take a holiday from the rat race. I told Graeme and Ross about my job, glamorizing it a bit, mentioning casually all the places we went on business trips—not telling them that all I saw of these places was the airports and the insides of hotels.

It was better when we spoke of the old days, of sliding down the hay till the backs of our legs were sore, of swimming in the icy-cold river, of picking brambles on a warm September afternoon.

When it was time to go, Graeme escorted me out to my car, elbowing Ross out of the way.

"Let me take you out to dinner tomorrow night, Alison. There's quite a decent place opened up in the town."

I said I'd be delighted.

Next morning I slept late, and when I came down Jill said that Ross had called in.

"He makes a point of calling in on me every day at some point to see if I've heard from Andrew. At least that's what he says, but really it's to make sure I'm all right and not fretting. He doesn't stay long, of course, in case of gossip."

"But surely no one would notice how long he stayed."

She looked at me with an amused expression.

"You're joking. However, they'll be too busy just now, discussing you."

I laughed. "I've been too long in London, where nobody bothers about you."

As I went out, she called after me, "Don't be late getting back for your date with Graeme."

I hadn't said anything about that. I wondered who had told her.

Graeme arrived in good time, looking as handsome as ever. He exchanged friendly banter with Jill, and I noticed that she, too, responded to his charm.

The "quite decent place" was very good indeed, the food excellent, and Graeme was a wonderful companion. I enjoyed it all, but when he wanted to take me on to the Rugby Club to meet some of his friends, I refused, pleading tiredness. Why, I didn't really know. I got the impression that he wanted to show me off, which was flattering. But I didn't want to be regarded as a trophy.

He would have kissed me when he took me home, but I slid out of the car quickly and said "Thank you" and "Good night" before he could. He looked distinctly put out.

Sleep was a long time in coming. I had wanted to fall in love as my grandfather and grandmother did, completely and utterly, excluding all others, and instinct had brought me back here. But instinct had proved wrong. Graeme wasn't capable of that kind of love. Pleasant, charming, but no depth to him. A love affair with him would be a happy, bubbly one with no scars that showed when it was over, but that was not for me. Not any longer. I decided to spend the rest of my holiday somewhere else.

In the morning Jill had a letter from her husband at last and was in high spirits. I was trying to get around to the subject of my departure when Ross arrived. In spite of the fact that it promised to be a fine day, he was wearing a duffel coat and heavy boots.

"Going somewhere?" I asked, eyebrows raised.

"Up on the hills, I'll bet," said Jill. "With the boys that are left behind."

"Well, they get a bit bored with the others away in Switzerland. It keeps them out of mischief."

"I wouldn't mind a bit of hill-walking myself," I said. "Remember father used to take us when he came on holiday?"

"Well, why don't you go?" Jill said.

Ross looked doubtfully at my cotton dress and open-toed sandals. "Not unless you've got something more suitable to wear."

"Of course I have. And I brought a pair of good stout walking shoes, too."

I flew upstairs, a bit nettled by the coolness of his manner and determined to show him. When he saw me in trousers and shirt, with an anorak Jill lent me, he had to admit I was adequately dressed, but he still didn't seem particularly enthusiastic about taking me.

The boys were more appreciative, though, when we met up with them. There was a wolf whistle or two and a bit of nudging and winking. Ross introduced me calmly. They were all about fourteen or fifteen and some of them were taller than I was.

"Ever been up in the hills afore, miss?" asked Billy,

or was it Hugh, pushing someone else aside to walk beside me.

"Not for a long time, but I don't expect it's changed much."

Nor had it. The rolling moorlands stretched before us as they had before our ancestors. The hills reached up into the sky, rejecting our voices as an intrusion on the silence. The crystal clear air was invigorating, and I strode out happily, knowing that tomorrow my legs would ache, but not caring.

Presently the boys raced ahead, competing with one another. Ross fell back beside me.

"Enjoying it?" he asked without his usual warm smile.

"Oh, yes. I'd forgotten how good it feels."

"I thought you would probably be too tired after your night out yesterday."

"We weren't late. As a matter of fact, I was thinking of leaving today until you talked me into this."

He ignored the banter and stopped, making me turn to face him.

"But why, Alison? Why would you want to leave when you've only just come back? Was it something Graeme did? Tell me."

He looked so worried I was touched. "Of course not. Graeme was the essence of charm, as I expect he is to every girl. I just felt like going somewhere else, that's all."

After a moment he relaxed and smiled at me. Things were back to normal between us again. He took my hand and we ran after the boys.

All morning we walked and climbed and sometimes stopped, breathless, to admire the view. We had lunch beside a stream that fell like a frill of white lace from the hills, and I was glad of the rest. Even the boys sat or lay about on the grass, chaffing one another and asking questions of Ross. It was obvious they liked and respected him. His manner was just right: he did not talk down to them, but did not try too hard to be one of them, either. When they were cheeky he gave back as good as he got.

"Sir," Hugh said suddenly. "What's yon bird?"

I had noticed it myself, particularly its mewing cry. For some time it had been gliding in circles not far from us.

"That's a buzzard," Ross told him.

It circled again, lower, and this time came so close to us that we could see that the tips of its broad wings curved upward and that its tail was striped brown and white. Suddenly it swooped down and rose again, something in its claws, something that squealed piteously. Hugh ran at it, shouting. The big bird dropped its prey and glided off with an indignant cry. We saw Hugh bend to pick up a small, furry body and then turn toward us.

"It's a rabbit," he cried. "And it's still alive."

Ross went up and took it from him. It was a young rabbit and it was badly hurt. Ross turned away for a moment, and when he turned back the small body was still.

He looked at the boy and said, "It's better this way. It wouldn't have lived."

The other boys had gone on ahead, but Hugh stayed looking at the young rabbit in Ross's hands. His face was expressionless, but his throat worked as if he were trying to swallow past a lump in it, then he turned and dashed after the others. I saw the compassion on Ross's face as he laid the dead rabbit on the rough grass.

I saw his kindness, his sensitivity, his concern for others, all the qualities that went to make up this man. And suddenly I knew. My instinct had not been wrong. This was the man I loved and would love till the end of my days. Would he feel the same about me? I held my breath until he raised his eyes to mine, and I knew beyond doubt that he did.

"Alison!" he said in wonder.

I went into his arms.

There was a chorus of oohs and aahs from above, reminding us of our interested audience. We turned and walked up toward the boys, our arms around each other.

"Are you sir's girl?" asked one, pushing in beside us.

Ross and I spoke together.

"Yes!" we said.

3 | THE SMILE ON THE FACE OF MISS PRINGLE
BY ROMA GROVER

My friend Miss Pringle always says you can tell when a couple have declared their love. Being rather old-fashioned, she uses expressions like "declared their love." You can tell, she says, by the way they hold hands. Before a declaration of love, they just hold hands. Afterward, they swing their hands while walking. There's a big difference. And Miss Pringle is very observant.

Unless, she said, things have changed since her day. No, I assured her, love is the one thing that doesn't change. She breathed a visible sigh of relief that while the cost of living rose and standards fell, love, at least, remained constant. Not that you could expect Miss Pringle to know much about love, living alone and being elderly.

"I've never seen you and James holding hands," she said suddenly, looking at me through rimless spectacles, over piles of books stacked on her living-room table.

"No?" I countered. "Well...." I didn't remind her that love is not the only thing that is declared. War is, too. And I wouldn't hold hands with that great-nephew of hers for all the tea in China, to use another of Miss Pringle's phrases. She is my dear friend, and I visit her because she's a love, and having James Macether for a great-nephew is not her fault.

Of course, he often visits her at the same time but that, to me, is more penalty than pleasure. We work together, and I see too much of him during the week to want his company at weekends.

To be more precise, I work for James Macether. He's the boss of Macether Antiques, a small bow-fronted shop tucked away in an alcove at the quiet end of the High Street. He does the buying and I do the selling, so you could say we are on opposite sides. When I can't sell the ugly rubbish he buys, he tells me I have no sales technique and then I tell him...well, never mind what I tell him. Let's just say we don't see eye to eye.

"I just don't know why you are so cool toward him," Miss Pringle said in the tone of voice that turns a statement into a question.

I could have given her three very good reasons. Sylvia, Bernice and Rosie. Impossible to find three better reasons than that. I didn't know them personally, of course. To me, the dogsbody who answered the phone, they were disembodied voices asking, frequently, if they could speak to James, please? Bernice said it with a sigh; she sounded sultry. Sylvia with a lighthearted giggle that suggested she and James shared many lighthearted giggles. And Rosie, well, I couldn't quite place Rosie. She sounded the quiet, serious type. I didn't intend to join the queue.

"No," I said to Miss Pringle. "We never hold hands."

Avoiding her gaze, I looked through the window at autumn taking place outside. I have to admit this is another reason I liked to visit Miss Pringle's cottage on the edge of rolling downland, a short walk from the sea. The seasons are not just dates on a desk calendar. They happen, and can be felt and witnessed. Take spring: it's all around you, a budding and a hopefulness that comes with the morning dew and progresses naturally to summer. And summer: that's the time when children carrying buckets and spades pass the cottage door, and evenings are touched by soft winds from the sea and a blackbird's song from the hedgerow.

I turned from the view and found Miss Pringle watching me searchingly over her wall of books.

"He's very fond of you, Harriet."

"Nonsense."

"Yes, he is," she said firmly. "I've watched him when you are together. I remember a poem...." Pausing, she searched her memory. "The first line went something like 'How closely I have come to loving you' and another line is, 'But you delayed a second's space and then....'" The trouble with you, Harriet, is that you run away from love."

"And the trouble with you, Miss Pringle," I replied with mock severity, "is that you are incurably romantic."

She stood up, "Very well. We'll have a cup of tea and talk about something else."

"Your ancestors," I suggested.

"My ancestors," she agreed.

Miss Pringle's ancestors were the reason she was

surrounded by books. She was tracing her family tree. "My great-nephew, James, collects antiques. I collect antique people," she once explained.

It began two years ago when she came across handwritten entries on the flyleaf of an old family Bible. The pages were yellowed with age, the ink faded, and we had read with difficulty, she and I, a little chronicle of Victorian babies, Joseph and George and Alice listed with their dates and times of birth.

"Such a pity we no longer follow this custom," she said. "And this one—" Her finger stopped at the name Abraham. "This one became my grandfather." She smiled, then frowned a little, trying to equate her memory of a bewhiskered old gentleman sitting at the head of the table leading family grace with the entry in the Bible, "March 2, 1861, 9:30 P.M., 7 lb. 2 oz."

The kettle steamed and boiled on the hob. That was another thing I liked about Miss Pringle's. Nothing changed, except the seasons. She had grown old, ignoring central heating and electric kettles, and a fire always burned in the grate. While she busied herself with teacups and bread and butter, Miss Pringle told about a recently discovered Scottish ancestor, Hamish Mactavish, who rallied his troops in a northern battle, stood on a rock sounding the advance and died not long afterward.

"Probably from pneumonia," Miss Pringle added. "Caught while standing on that rock, you know." She sighed again. "A fine figure of a man."

Not that Miss Pringle possessed evidence of his fine figure. It was just that all her male ancestors conformed to a high standard of masculinity, being upright, courageous, handsome, learned, patriotic, unfailing in the line of duty but tender and protective toward the fair sex. Oh, yes, they knew what was expected of them.

Sometimes I wondered how Miss Pringle's family tree managed to produce its latest male offshoot, namely James Macether. Hardly a fine figure of a man, though I suppose given the right situation, the challenging circumstances, yes, I suppose it was just possible....

But no, James would not go down in the Macether family history as the one who led a regiment to victory or the one who restored the family fortune with a lucky throw of dice. He'd be remembered as the one who needed six hands in order to cope with Sylvia, Bernice and Rosie. I sometimes wondered if his love life ever overlapped.

After tea, I kissed Miss Pringle goodbye and walked down the path, leaving her outlined in yellow light in the doorway.

"Give my love to James," she called, and waved.

A mist crept in from the sea and autumn dusk surrounded the spinney. It was beautiful.

Autumn was doing its best in town, too. Golden-leafed trees cast shadows on the pavement outside the shop. On Monday morning I unlocked the door and went inside and reveled for a few minutes in the pervading antique shop smell; the musty smell of a row of Victorian chairs, the upholstery shaped by the attitudes of unknown sitters and still listening, it seemed, to Victorian conversation. And of polish once diligently applied to a mahogany table that supported many sepia photographs of young men in uniform: husbands and brothers and sweethearts, who had once gone to war, and who now watched over a silent weekend shop. I hoped James would be able to sell the chairs soon. We needed a good sale to balance the books.

In the window, autumn sunlight glinted through Victorian glassware: charming, pink Bristol glass and dishes with rainbows of color. The kind they used to give away as prizes at fairgrounds.

I moved an aspidistra pedestal of singular ugliness, as it was taking too much window space. That's James's taste for you. Awful.

I turned, and Shadow, our white kitten, ran across the shop to greet me, so I knew James had arrived. We took turns looking after Shadow on weekends, just as we did to visit Miss Pringle. James one Sunday—me, the next. At least we had Miss Pringle and Shadow in common.

Shadow, whose contribution to the shop was to lie in feline slumber on a chaise longue in the window, purred against my neck as I carried her to the back room where James kept the filing cabinets, ledgers, kettle and milk. I met him.

"Did you see Aunt Jessica yesterday?" he asked, no doubt to divert attention from the monstrosity he was trying to lever through the open door. It looked like half a Viking ship, complete with candleholders, mirrors and drawers.

"Yes."

"How was she?"

"All right," I said. "Busy." On second thought, it reminded me of an ugly sideboard with a ship's figurehead at one end. It was the kind of female figurehead they used to attach to the prow of a ship to ward off the evil eye.

"James, what is it? That thing?"

He stopped to unhook his waistcoat buttonhole from

the knob of a drawer. If there is a time when I warm to James, and I only say if, then it's when he's moving furniture. Being a naturally elegant man, streamlined wrists and tall, with a nice head and dark hair growing close to his neck, he looks like a poet who is unexpectedly called to hump sacks of coal. Sort of outraged and vulnerable. Almost human, in fact. And he always manages to become hooked on something.

"It will take more than clever salesmanship to sell that thing," I went on.

"That—" he straightened and gave me a fearless look a man gives a woman when he thinks she is being foolish "—is not one thing, it's two things. Someone in years gone by, for a reason known only to himself, nailed the two together. Don't just stand there, woman. Come and help."

We brought the monstrosity inside, but it wasn't easy. James stopped to wipe his forehead, then lovingly ran a hand along the sideboard. Suddenly I knew how that hand would feel in a gently loving touch. I wished...but no, no point in wishing! That touch was reserved for furniture. Now if I were an old sideboard...or even Sylvia, Bernice or Rosie perhaps.

"What kind of idiot could want to drive nails in such beautiful wood?" he asked, his hand moving back and forth along the grain.

Personally, I preferred the figurehead with her fierce stare and carved curls flowing forever in a sea wind. And that wooden aristocratic nose that must have pioneered many pathways through unchartered waters. But then James and I have nothing in common. Apart from mutual affection for Miss Pringle and Shadow, of course.

In answer to his question, I said, "Probably an old sea captain who wanted to keep the evil eye off his bacon and eggs."

"Get to your work, woman." James gave me a glare that could only have been inherited from a long line of aggressive, conquering, male chauvinist ancestors.

The ping of the shop bell left no choice, and I sold an elaborate Edwardian hatpin to a man wearing jeans and a beard, who said he wanted the pin to clean the keys of his typewriter. That's what I call style. Not at all like James's sartorial image. A glance through the doorway between shop and office showed James white-cuffed and impeccably tailored, trying to disentangle sideboard and figurehead.

"Ugly, isn't she?" he said when he had completed his task.

"No, I don't think so. Not as ugly as something else I could mention." I glanced at the sideboard, and then began to apply cleaning fluid to the face of Miranda. Somehow we called her that. It suited her. "Look, the colors are still bright."

And they were. The painted skin tones and copper-colored ringlets glowed. The eyes, woodenly staring, were ringed in black paint, while the lips, a bright red, were carved to a perpetual half smile. An enigmatic smile, as if she knew what lay behind the next sunset. I wondered how many oceans she had pioneered, guarding her ship and crew. "How old is she, James? Can you fix a date?"

He considered for a moment. "Old. Very old. And ugly."

We worked late that evening, long after the shop was closed.

"What about coming with me for some supper,

Harriet?" James lifted Miranda and placed her in the window. It seemed an ignominious end, doomed to stare across the High Street after a life of adventure on the high seas. "The Chinese restaurant will be open." He looked at me, his voice soft, endearing, so why didn't I accept?

"No, I don't think so. Thank you all the same."

Running away again, Miss Pringle would have accused. Afraid to get involved. Of course, I knew the real reasons. We had nothing to talk about, James and I, and besides, being my boss, he might one day fire me. In fact, if the credit column did not improve soon, he would have to fire me. "I thought I'd have an early night."

"As you wish," he said, and turned away to find his coat.

I fed Shadow, and I can remember now the strange silence that filled the shop. A street light sent shadows dancing across Miranda's face, carving anew the high nose and mysterious smile.

"Lock up when you've finished," James called from the door. "Good night, Harriet."

The next day James received an offer for Miranda. A good offer, and he refused it. I couldn't believe it at first.

"But why?" I asked when the customer had left. "A sale like that would balance the books. Why did you say she had been sold?"

"Because I have plans for her." He leaned an elbow on a Victorian whatnot. "I've been doing some research into the family tree, and I think Aunt Jessica would be interested in Miranda."

"Miss Pringle?" I suppose I sounded surprise. "But— do you care about her research?"

"Of course I care. Get to your work, woman."

I turned to answer the shop bell. "Well, it's your turn to visit this weekend. Give Miss Pringle my love."

But the next day she phoned to ask us to go together. Come on Saturday evening, stay the night, stay for Sunday lunch, she said, adding she had something to tell us.

"Seems we'll have to tolerate each other for a short weekend," James remarked, replacing the telephone receiver.

"Seems we will," I agreed.

Then he turned and said, almost shyly, "Besides, I need Miranda for tonight's evening class. Why don't you come along to my class on the appreciation of antiques. It's wood carvings tonight, primitive tribal carvings. You never know, you might learn something. At the Education Center. You know where it is? Eight sharp."

"I'll think about it," I said. No doubt Sylvia, Bernice and Rosie would have jumped at the chance, but I just thought about it and eventually the idea of watching James trying to justify his bad taste began to appeal to me.

The class had already started when I arrived, and I crept sheepishly to the back row. James and Miranda occupied a table at the front, and I sat down and looked them both in the eye. Miranda loomed rather large and bestowed a disdainful smile, as well she might, on the ugliest collection of wood carvings I had ever seen. Carvings of skulls and strange birds and little men with short legs and large heads. Goodness knows where James found them.

"Now this one—" he picked up the most grotesque

carving and passed it to two middle-aged ladies sitting in the front row "—was made by a tribe that once lived in the rain forests of South America. Perhaps you can tell us something about it, Bernice? Or you, Sylvia?" he invited. I could scarcely believe it.

Surely those two comfortable ladies could not be Sylvia and Bernice. Surely not, but they were. And it seemed safe to assume that the elderly lady sitting next to them was Rosie. She was like an antique herself. A nice little Victorian antique, well-upholstered and lived-in and mellowed, and she brought some delicious homemade fudge that we ate during the tea break.

"I hope you have learned one or two things," James remarked pleasantly when the class was over.

"Oh, I have," I agreed, and if Miranda hadn't been so aristocratic and aloof, I swear she would have given me a sly wink.

The next time I saw Miranda we were all on our way to see Miss Pringle.

We left on Saturday evening, after closing time, James impeccably sweatered and jeaned, Shadow protesting in a basket, Miranda on the back seat, and me feeling relaxed and strangely at ease with James. Tolerating him might not prove too difficult after all.

After an unusually warm day for autumn, the colors of the evening were muted by mist. We drove in silence until the wind blew from the sea to greet us, salty and smelling of freedom.

James stopped the car outside the gate, pulling up on the grass verge. Turning, he took my hand, kissed it and smiled. "Tolerating you has been a pleasure," he said.

We got out and walked along the path, opened the

front door, which was always unlatched, and found the cottage to be empty. The table was set with three places, the fire banked for her return, but there was no sign of Miss Pringle.

"What now?" I looked around the dim room and then at James, aware of gathering dusk.

"Strange," he said. "She knew we would arrive about this time. I know—the beach. She's gone for an evening walk. Come on."

He took my hand and we went out and along the lane, walking to the sound of the sea.

The sunset spilled red on the incoming tide. Rocks cast purple shadows. The slight wind blew chill. James scanned the bay, from one outcrop of rocks to another, then his gaze swept along the empty beach. Close by, someone had written in the sand. The tide swilled forward and back, dragging half the message to nothing so that only "I lov ou" remained.

"If I weren't so worried about Aunt Jessica, I'd rewrite it—for you. I'll do it later."

The tenderness in his voice made me look at him quickly. This was a James I didn't know. I wanted to say, "Rewrite it now," but the sound of Miss Pringle's voice interrupted.

"James! Harriet!" The voice carried across water. "I'm here. On the rock. Out in the bay."

And there she was, a small upright figure waving a notebook, her gray coat blending with the rock that was, I judged quickly, about thirty yards from the beach. That rock, I knew, was never covered, not even in a high winter tide. Nevertheless, the water raced and glittered in the evening sun, and looked dangerous.

"Well," James said resignedly, "I suppose I must rescue her."

"I suppose you must," I replied, and just after that, it happened. The feeling that comes over you that you know later as love...as James took off shoes and socks and I saw him wade out to sea to rescue Miss Pringle. He scooped her off the rock and carried her back and set her down on dry sand, both of them soaking wet.

"Try not to do that again, love. Okay?"

"Yes, dear." Miss Pringle smiled up at him. "But I discovered that our ancestors came by sea. Around that point there." Her arms stretched vaguely toward the horizon. "They invaded."

"Yes, I know. I discovered that too. And we've brought you the wooden figurehead from the ship they sailed. Well, probably sailed," he qualified. "We've brought her to you, Harriet and I, and back to the sea where she belongs."

"Oh, how kind," Miss Pringle murmured, squeezing water from the hem of her coat. "You and Harriet. Well, well."

And on her face was a little smile identical to Miranda's, as if they both knew what lay behind the next sunset.

"Come on," I said. "You both need towels." After all, somebody had to be practical.

James took my hand, and we walked back to the cottage. There were one or two questions I wanted to ask Miss Pringle, later when she was dry and warm, such as how she allowed herself to be marooned on a rock when she was familiar with every turn of the tide. But that could wait until I had asked her if there was still room for another entry in her family Bible, a few more additions to the family tree.

4 | WHEN WINTER COMES
BY MAUREEN LEE

Samantha thought the summer would never end. Long golden days merged into one, so that she couldn't remember where she and Luke had been on any particular day. Was it Tuesday or Wednesday they'd gone to the beach party? Who knew? Who cared?

She awoke each morning to a room flooded with sunlight and, while she dressed, watched the boats already at sea. They bobbed across the bay, where the turquoise waves were fringed with frills of white surf. The whole scene was topped by the blue, the never-ending blue of the sky, where the sun, like a blinding jewel, shone day after day.

The visitors kept coming, and Samantha's mother was still busy providing bed and breakfast and evening meals weeks after the season usually ended. Samantha, who had finished university in July, stayed at home to help instead of going off into the great, wide world to seek her fortune.

It was really for Luke she stayed. He had finished a three-year contract in oil-rich Saudi Arabia earlier in the year and, being free, had offered to look after his aunt's tiny antique shop near the quay. Samantha had met him when she went in to ask the price of a small painting of the town at the turn of the century.

The figure had dismayed them both but they laughed about it, and he had asked her out and they had kept on laughing about something or other for the whole summer.

They went swimming in the sea at midnight, the warm waves lapping over their brown bodies; danced on the pier, at clubs, in discos; went to shows, watched dolphins, rode in seaplanes and sailing boats, and life became one long web of magic that consisted only of Luke and herself and sunlight, music and laughter.

Soon it would end, in one way or another. One morning she would awake to find a clouded sky, a chill in the air and winter on its way.

But not yet. Samantha refused to think about it. Tonight they were going to a party. They had become a pair. Samantha and Luke.

She made beds in a dream, helped her mother wash dishes, making mechanical conversation. Her mother gave her a sharp glance.

"You're going to come down to earth with a bump, my girl," she said dryly.

Samantha glanced at her in amusement. "I shall come down to earth on top of you," she answered, smiling at her mother's ample form. "And you shall cushion my fall."

Her mother couldn't resist smiling back. Samantha's happiness was infectious.

"Will you go to the library for me this morning, dear?" she asked. "Your father wants that new book on the Duke of Wellington, and you know how he must get his request in before Mr. Courtney."

Samantha's father was a keen amateur historian, and vied with another inhabitant of the town with the same interest in being the first to get newly published books from the library.

Tying a scarf over her long tangle of nut-brown hair, Samantha stepped out into the sunlit street. It was still early enough for the air to smell salty, and she could hear the faint hiss and rustle of the tide coming in.

She swung her bag of books as she walked along to the library, unconscious of the admiring glances at her lithe, slim figure in T-shirt and jeans. Her blue eyes glowed with happiness, and she wanted to laugh aloud for no reason at all.

Through the small thick panes of the antique-shop window she could see Luke dealing with a customer, an old lady examining china. He saw Samantha and waved and blew kisses over the old lady's head. His brown eyes gleamed with merriment and love.

She imagined his sunburned hands holding her that night when they danced. Afterward on top of the hill, they would stop the car as they always did, and look down at the town lights and the moon reflected in the still, still ocean, and he would kiss her and the moment would become sheer bliss.

In the library Samantha met Donald Mackay, the new librarian. She had come to know him quite well in a short time; he was unmarried, she knew, because he lodged with one of her mother's friends until he could find something more permanent. He was fair-haired, and when he talked about his beloved books a boyish grin would light up his face.

"You're too late," he said when she handed in a request card. "Will Courtney's already asked for it." He knew about the feud between the two men.

Samantha grimaced. "Never mind. Dad just can't bear to think of another person learning something new about history before he does."

"Are you doing anything tonight, Samantha?" Donald asked shyly. "There's a good film on at the Piaza."

He didn't mix with the local young crowd much. Didn't know about Samantha and Luke, who were a pair.

But something stopped Samantha from mentioning Luke. She could never, in a million years, have said what it was.

Instead of refusing outright as she knew she should have done, she said, "I'm frightfully busy this week. Besides, I've already seen the film. But maybe some other time."

Donald Mackay looked pleased and vaguely wished he was dishonest enough to put Samantha's father first on the list for the book on the Duke of Wellington. But he wasn't, and he didn't think Samantha would appreciate the gesture anyway. . . .

The party was marvelous: lights softly dimmed, sweet music, lots of friends and Samantha and Luke, the perfect couple, locked in each other's arms, dancing as one person for most of the evening.

Samantha, eyes closed, thought, *this will go on for ever and ever and ever. I shall not forget this moment as long as I live.* But then, she had said those same words to herself so many times during that wonderful summer.

They stopped on the hill outside town. Luke leaned over and took her in his arms, and she caressed the dark curls on the nape of his neck. Their lips met, and Samantha's heart gave its old, familiar lurch.

The next night there was a champagne supper with some other antique dealers. The night after that, she and Luke went to dinner, just the two of them, to a little Greek restaurant. They ate moussaka and sipped unfamiliar retsina, accompanied by haunting music from a group of musicians.

"Samantha, Samantha," whispered Luke as he kissed her that night. "I love you, darling."

And Samantha replied with fervor, as she usually did, that she loved him, too.

The following morning, Samantha had no idea what day of the week it was.

"When does Luke go back?" her mother asked.

"Back where?" her daughter asked dreamily.

"To wherever he comes from," her mother snapped.

"He comes from nowhere, really. His parents are dead," Samantha explained softly. "He was at school and university until he was twenty-one, then in Saudi Arabia for three years. He can stay wherever he likes. Here, if he wants to."

"Does he want to?" her mother asked, frowning. "And do you want him to?"

"I don't know." Samantha's eyes opened wide in surprise. "I don't suppose he knows, either. We hadn't thought about it."

Her mother looked worried. "Isn't it about time you did?" she asked. "Everything's been too perfect for you. Love is one thing, marriage another. Marriage isn't perfect. Marriage is comforting someone when they're ill, wiping their brow and washing their clothes."

Her mother was upset, concerned lest her daughter plunge into marriage believing it would be a continuation of the fairy-tale relationship she'd basked in all summer. "Marriage is changing diapers and crying children. How would your Luke cope with them?"

"I've no idea," Samantha admitted honestly. She sat down at the kitchen table and thought deeply, and her mother said nothing more.

It was impossible, absolutely impossible, to envisage Luke ill in bed or struggling to change a baby's diaper. She remembered the way her own father had walked the floor at night with her young brother when he was a baby and had awful teething trouble. With Luke you laughed and sang, swam in a moon-gilded sea, danced and kissed, you didn't do the....

Samantha stopped herself. She had just been about to add the "real" things in life. But everything was real—in its own way. Could she and Luke help it that things had not gone wrong? Besides, they hadn't mentioned marriage, either of them. There'd been no need.

She shook her head impatiently. Why bother thinking about it? Tonight was yet to come, and that was all that mattered. She laughed aloud when she thought about it.

Upstairs, her mother heard the laugh and sighed.

The jazz club was in the cellar of a pub in the next

town. They met stacks of people they knew and stayed until the early hours of the morning.

Luke stopped the car in the usual place on the way home and reached out his arms for her.

"Don't!" said Samantha, surprising herself.

"What's the matter?" he asked, bewildered.

"I don't know."

She shivered, then said, "Luke, the water isn't so blue."

"It was bound to change sometime." He shrugged.

Samantha turned and buried her head in his shoulder, and he held her tightly for a long time.

The next morning she awoke and sleepily wondered for a few seconds what was wrong with her bedroom. Her heart sank when she realized the sky was gray, and the room looked strange without the sunlight streaming in. It seemed as though the whole world had changed.

As she dressed she watched one lone fishing boat struggling across the choppy brown water of the bay.

Her mother looked sad as she put her daughter's breakfast before her. "Where are you going tonight?" she asked.

"We were going to a barbecue at Wrentford, but it'll be canceled if the weather doesn't improve," Samantha said with a sigh.

It didn't improve. In fact, it got worse and when Luke called for her that night it was raining and he looked unfamiliar in a rather crumpled old raincoat.

They went for a drink in a local pub, which was nearly empty because it was Friday, and the remaining holiday visitors had decided to go home instead of hanging about in the wet until the following day.

Samantha and Luke were strangely silent. Everything that had been between them seemed to have belonged to the sunshine and the warm sea, to joy and laughter.

But, in this shabby little pub, what was there to say to each other? Samantha could think of nothing, and she was glad when Donald Mackay walked in, a couple of books under his arm.

He grinned when he saw them and asked if he could sit at their table. Samantha was ashamed of the alacrity with which she agreed and couldn't help noticing Luke looked relieved at the arrival of the newcomer.

"I expect you'll be packing up soon," Donald said after a while, and Luke nodded.

"This weekend, probably," he said.

Samantha felt her heart miss a beat. She tried to look politely interested.

"Where will you go?" asked Donald.

Luke toyed with the handle of his glass and looked vague. "I've no idea. It depends on a lot of things."

The pub wasn't far from Luke's shop. All three left together and when they were outside, Samantha said, "There's no need to walk home with me, Luke. Donald lives only a few doors away."

"As you wish," he answered stiffly, and turning abruptly, he walked down the street, shoulders hunched against the rain, looking downcast and miserable—nothing like the dashing, romantic young man who had wooed her all summer.

Why had she done that? Deliberately hurt him? Samantha was angry with herself but knew it was because she didn't want to be alone with him. Somehow, it was easier to talk to Donald.

Back home, all the family were in bed and she sat in

the kitchen until the early hours of the morning, drinking endless cups of coffee, eyes burning, wanting to cry, yet not able to.

How would she feel if she went to Luke's shop in the morning and he'd gone? Her breath drew in sharply at the mere thought. Surely, it would break her heart. Would it? She didn't know.

Rising from the table to make yet more coffee, she was startled by the ringing of the phone and rushed into the hall to answer it before it woke her parents.

"Samantha?"

It was Luke.

She mumbled something incoherent.

"Samantha, I'm sorry to ring at such a stupid time, but I can't sleep."

"Neither can I," she confessed.

"Look, I've been thinking. I was going to pack tonight, and leave first thing in the morning." His voice cracked a little. "Samantha, are you listening?"

"Of course," she almost sobbed.

"But I don't want to. At least, I'm pretty sure I don't want to. Do you want me to leave, Samantha?" How different was his voice from the firm, laughing tones she'd heard all summer.

"I'm pretty sure I don't want you to," she answered softly. "But we'll have to meet and talk and then, maybe...."

"I'll come first thing in the morning. Well, today, in fact. It's nearly two."

"Today. Yes, come today," she said, and put the receiver down and leaned back against the wall with a sigh of relief.

Maybe they'd just got off to a more marvelous start than most people. Maybe they'd have to get to know each other all over again, in the ordinary way other people did. He would come tomorrow, no, today. Then, maybe....

Her eyes glowed, and she went upstairs to bed with a light step, murmuring to herself, "Maybe."

5 | FARMER JO
BY FRANCES MELVIN

I thrust the big fork into the soil and leaned upon it thoughtfully. I was remembering—as one does, at the most unkind moments—my airy replies to those of my city friends who had exclaimed in horror over my giving up my job in advertising to run a farm. What on earth would I do with myself, they'd wondered.

"Why—float around in pretty smock dresses," I had said—admittedly in fun. "Pick mushrooms on dewy mornings. Collect warm brown eggs in a basket."

I had had about twenty-odd months in which to eat my words.

It was a bitter March morning, and the remains of a sea fog clung lovingly to the half acre of cabbages I was in the process of uprooting. Over my three jumpers I wore a waterproof against the cold wet air. Through the thinning fog I could see a sun about as big and warm as a snowball. Down at my feet, I could see that my cabbages had clubroot. The memory of those frivolous days in town was like gall and worm-wood, as the phrase has it.

To make matters worse, I was suddenly disturbed by the sound of a Land Rover on the track behind me; it screeched to a halt and the usual unwelcome voice floated over the field. "You're up early. Couldn't you sleep?"

I stood motionless. I looked such a freak, maybe he'd think I was one of my own scarecrows and drive on.

No such luck. He climbed out of his vehicle and came striding over the hard soil to me. I turned and surveyed him without pleasure.

"Ah—you're alive," he said casually. "You were so still I thought you'd frozen into a solid block. Aha...." He went down on his haunches and surveyed the telltale smears on the stem and roots of my cabbages. "D'you know you've got clubroot?" he inquired cheerfully. He was in a good mood.

"Yes," I replied grimly. "I can still use them, though."

He shook his head mournfully. "I think you're going to lose the profit on this crop."

"Yes. I'd realized that ten minutes ago. Good morning."

"Did you dig in any lime before you planted? Have you used anything on them since?"

I closed my eyes and sought patience. "Yes, to both questions. I'm sure you're very busy, so—"

He stood up to his full six feet. His eyes sparkled with pleasurable menace. "Still refuse to be beaten, eh, Joanna?"

I smiled thinly and opened my eyes. "Go away," I said with tremendous restraint. He gave a throaty laugh and tugged my bush hat over my eyes. Then he was on his way, and I found myself breathing more easily. Samuel Alderson, dairy farmer and cereal grower, alias the Arch Enemy, was having a bad effect on my blood pressure, I was sure.

His farm covered several hundred acres of pasture and arable land, and it bordered my small holding of a few acres on the east. He had two farm cottages on his property, and the men who inhabited them were young, healthy and able. He had a brand-new tractor and efficient-looking accoutrements that gleamed, and a combine harvester that could have won prizes. His cow byre was of the five-star variety, with a slatted hard rubber floor to keep the cows' feet warm in winter.

On the other side of the hawthorn hedge, I had a contraption that could have been a tractor or the front of an old bus, a rusty plough and one or two other accessories that just about worked. I had spasmodic help from a couple of taciturn characters who assisted other smallholders and market gardeners in the area, and I had Percy, the vegetable man, to relieve me of my produce and sell it in the neighboring town and villages.

The Arch Enemy had a thriving herd of Jerseys, Friesians and a Hereford-cross bull.

I had Tatiana, and it was not funny, having a venerable cow whose shoulder blades pushed through her aged hide.

All this, plus a sizable chicken run and a crumbling house, was bequeathed to me almost two years ago by my Uncle George, and it was about the strangest thing a relative of mine has ever done.

A lot of the family said that Uncle George had gone

a bit peculiar in his old age. To me, this had sounded extremely unfair. After all, I had kept in touch with him over the years and, in my childhood had spent many a happy holiday at Martin's Beck. Mind, that had been years ago, when Auntie Lea was alive and the house and fields had been a children's paradise of crooked stairs and secret hiding places. Uncle George had never had children, and before he died he had had neither the impetus nor the physical strength to keep up with the pace of twentieth-century agriculture. The others in the family had grown up and gone away to places that were more cosmopolitan or simply more beautiful than Martin's Beck.

I myself had sought the bright lights. My parents had settled overseas some years ago, and I'd been working successfully in advertising when the news of the inheritance had come; everyone expected me to sell. Who would want to go and live in the back of beyond, they said. The farm is way up in the north, about fifteen miles from the sea, in a place known to the locals as Martin's Beck, which is near to a place called Maweston, which isn't near anywhere at all.

They were all astounded when I announced my intentions. It was a complete reversal of the life expected of a girl today. "Two years," I declared. "Give me two years and I'll make a commercial success of it."

So, the office clubbed together and bought me a set of large gardening tools, and presented them to me at a farewell party in a smart French restaurant in Soho. *She's mad*, I could see them musing to themselves.

Sometimes, in the months that followed, I had felt inclined to agree. As I leaned on the fork from that very gardening set, staring moodily at my stunted cabbages, I was aware of a more frightening possibility. Financial disaster.

The day I had arrived at Martin's Beck had been cold, blustery and clear; I was very aware of the mixture of pungent scents that prevails in the air close to the sea. It had been late afternoon, and as I turned off the main road to the "farm," I felt a tremor of nervousness.

When I saw the house, the slate roof bowed with age, the windows empty and staring, I was temporarily struck dumb at the idiocy of my wild ambitions. Run this place? Myself?

I climbed out of my Mini and huddled inside my furry jacket; a streak of pale gold lit the sky and reflected in a shimmering puddle at my feet. I went toward the cluster of outbuildings. I had on Italian leather boots with high heels that kept sinking in the peaty soil. The house and livestock had been looked after by neighbors, I had been assured, so the chickens in the run were fed, the outbuildings barred and padlocked. The wind sang over the grasses and round the sheds. It seemed daunting and lonely. *Right*, I decided, *you win*, and was making for the car and thoughts of the city, when a man's voice hailed me.

I stopped. He was striding round the side of the house in waders and a battle jacket, tall and smiling. "You must be old George's niece," he said, coming alongside me. "Poor old George." He looked me up and down, still smiling, and I did not think he was referring to the state of my late uncle's finances.

I smiled brightly back. What nerve, I thought. "That's right. His niece, Joanna Halsall. And you are...?"

"Alderson. Sam Alderson. Your neighbor. I own

Beck Farm. See the house over by the far clump of trees? I saw you drive up—one doesn't miss much in this place—so I came over to say hello. You were walking back to your car—?"

"Yes, I—"

"Forgotten the keys to the house? I thought as much."

"No, I—"

"I've got the spares. Better come in and get warm," he advised, with a derisory glance at my clothes that were fashion's idea of country wear. "Now, if you want me or Winnie, who lives over at Old Beck's Rise, to go on looking after the place, we'll be glad to. How long are you staying? Long enough to put the house to rights?"

"Mr. Alderson, you ought to know that—"

"In you go!" He had the front door open and I hesitated, annoyed, before stepping into the old house. There had been a scent of distant familiarity: something to do with children's sunny summers, the smell of baking in the kitchen, and Auntie Lea to kiss away the bruises....

Lino and carpet hid the stone floors now, and a brightly covered three-piece suite that sagged in all the comfy places stood in the sitting room.

"Not bad, is it? There isn't much to do, you see." Sam Alderson strode into the middle of the room.

"Come in," I said pointedly, but he just gave me his crooked-mouthed smile.

"I don't believe in beating about the bush, Miss Halsall, so I'll get straight to the point. I can make you a very good offer for this place, very good indeed. Better than you'd get from most, I should think, because these few acres could be valuable to me, situated right on my doorstep."

"Look, Mr. Alderson," I said quickly, "I have no intention of selling, thanks all the same. Uncle George left the—the farm to me, though quite why he did so I can't think."

"Precisely." My neighbor bowed his head solemnly. I saw red.

"But I don't mean to let it out of the family! I'm going to take up where he left off and—and—get things moving. Of course, I haven't inspected the property yet, and I've a lot to learn, but I've been reading up on things in London this past month. I'm willing and able, and I'll keep on Uncle George's farm workers. Yes—" I turned to him "—I mean to make it work."

Unfortunately this daring speech was brought to a close by a mournful and penetrating bellow that sounded from outside. I jumped. Sam Alderson appeared to be having difficulty keeping a straight face.

"That, er," he began. "That is Tatiana."

"I beg your pardon?"

"Your stock."

"My—?" It couldn't be...not the elderly red-and-white creature who had long since stopped giving more than a couple of gallons of milk a day...still alive? And that name! Oh yes. Uncle George and his wry Northern humor had a lot to answer for.

"What does she want?" I asked dumbly.

"A bit of company, probably. Old George was very fond of her. He used to come over and talk stock with me a couple of times a week. I told him he ought to get the butcher in—"

"How horrible!" I exclaimed feelingly. But another bellow sent us both out to the cow byre. I realized immediately that I would need time to get used to Tatiana.

I patted her rough neck and said a nervous hello, but when she swung her great head round it was all I could do to keep from jumping.

"George used to bring her over to my bull," Sam Alderson put in conversationally. "Will you be—?"

"I'll be looking things over," I said firmly.

Sam Alderson shrugged. "I'll be getting along, then. Winnie's stocked up your larder, and there's butter and milk from my place. I used to provide George with them in exchange for a few vegetables. I hope you grow as good sweet parsnips as he did." His smile took on newer dimensions of skepticism. I lifted my chin.

"I'll do my best, Mr. Alderson. After all, I was born in the country, you know, and they do say that if it's in your blood you're halfway there."

He nodded, considering. "Er, halfway to what?" he asked.

I narrowed my eyes. "Success, Mr. Alderson." I crossed my fingers behind my back.

"Righto." He turned and made for the door. "By the way, if you change your mind and decide to sell, I'll take that old bag of bones off your hands—"

"Goodbye, Mr. Alderson." But he only laughed, and left.

Round about then I labeled him the Arch Enemy. Each morning he would cruise by my plot atop his streamlined tractor, dismounting to dispense a lordly greeting or a rude remark, dependent on the nature of our relationship at each particular time. At first, picking my way delicately through the furrowed soil, I would attempt to keep face, and retort bravely or ignore him.

But time passed, and gradually I changed. Soon the faded jeans of my London life became Sunday wear, and I was out in serviceable waders myself, my blond hair tucked into a bush hat and my corduroys smeared with mud. If it was the last thing I did, I would think to myself, I'd give Sam Alderson a run for his money.

I went into Maweston and ordered the books on market gardening I didn't have already. The trouble was, I was far too independent to read them. I would sooner listen to my two laconic workmen who would give hints if asked, or, better still, Percy-the-veg-man who gave long informative addresses on crops, standing at my kitchen door in a gray shin-length overall with a stub of pencil behind his ear.

Whatever it was that caused such mulish determination on my part, I needed every ounce of it that first dreadful winter.

When heavy rains had ruined the remains of a turnip crop that I hadn't known ought to have been harvested, a howling north wind swept over the landscape and blew away a compost bin I'd constructed painstakingly from new wood. Snow fell in January and trickled its picturesque way through an unsuspected crack in my storage-shed roof, freezing several layers of potatoes that had been stored by Uncle George. This last, plus an hour or two up on the roof nailing down tarpaulin, and my thumb, over the hole, sent me indoors almost weeping with pain and frustration.

I was gingerly rubbing my frozen fingers in front of the range when there was a knock at the door. I opened it. Sam Alderson, in convivial mood, stood on the snow-trodden step.

Throbbing hands, potatoes, the cruel elements were forgotten. "No!" I said firmly. "And I mean it!"

He had, in fact, visited me a number of times under false pretences that only just obscured his desire to buy me out. Today he nodded amicably. "That's a pity. I would have thought you'd enjoy a night at the theater."

"Sorry?"

"I was given a couple of tickets for Maweston Rep. It's not exactly Shaftesbury Avenue, but...." He raised one eyebrow and regarded me quizzically.

"We-ell," I began with feigned reluctance, "I do have a lot on at the moment, but...."

He laughed sympathetically. "Of course you have. Well, maybe another time. Cheerio." He turned and strode down the path like a man who can take rejection. I was furious. The wretched fellow knew perfectly well I had been about to accept...then I thought of the way I'd greeted him and closed the door, my mind in turmoil.

Later that week one of my men went down with a stomach bug, and the manuring I hadn't done in autumn was delayed when the tractor broke down. Sam Alderson came calling.

"Having a day off?" he inquired rashly. "I saw your old bus gasping its last up there."

"Why is it," I demanded crossly, "that you always manage to call when something's just gone wrong? There are days when absolutely nothing happens, you know. Smooth, efficient days when the hens are laying perfectly. Now if you'll excuse me...."

He followed me out to the small shed where I kept things mechanical. I began hunting for a spanner, while the Arch Enemy leaned against the doorframe and watched me with inexplicable amusement.

Eventually he said, quite casually, "All right. You've

convinced me that you'd even try and fix that old boneshaker. In the meantime, do you want to borrow mine to get the job done?"

I was surprised into silence. Then immensely grateful. His was the Rolls-Royce of tractors, but he still helped mend the old engine of mine. . . .

By now I had gleaned some knowledge of agriculture. I had learned about crop rotation; I had learned that Tatiana was past the age of being taken to Sam Alderson's bull and only sheer sentimentality on my part kept her alive. I had discovered that I could replace a fuse, handle sacks of fertilizer and shout "Cush!" at cows and actually make them move. I had also found friends among the people living round and about. March and part of April went by in a whirlwind of sowing, fertilizing and planting that almost left me dizzy.

And when all the harsh blows hadn't defeated me, a small miracle happened.

The bite went out of the wind and the ponderous skies cleared; the fields were dusted with pale green, the pastures smelled rich and suddenly had lambs prancing about in them. A bleak tree that had stood outside my front door all winter revealed itself as a wild cherry and broke into thick, fragrant blossom. A warm breeze blew in from the west, and the air was alive with larks and the tang of the sea.

I stood at the kitchen door one morning with a mug of tea and a thick slice of toast and watched Tatiana grazing contentedly in the field by the road while smoke trailed idly from my various neighbors' chimney pots. The sun shone. In a far-off field a cloud of gulls followed the wake of Sam Alderson's tractor. And my crops were actually growing.

So it was that I had beaten the first year at Martin's Beck; the next had been slightly easier, and by now I knew that the farm was where I belonged. Yet I had very little money, and eking out a living was a constant headache.

The stunted cabbages of this morning were a good example of what could go wrong, although I could chalk up a sign announcing Home Grown Cabbages and put it at the side of the road with a giveaway price to attract motorist custom, as I had in the summer with fruit.

But that night, sitting in front of the fire with the accounts books spread before me, I recalled my promise before I left advertising: "Give me two years...." Of course, when Auntie Lea and Uncle George had been young they had kept several head of cattle, some pigs for market, more chickens. But it would be a near impossibility for me to build up a farm of that strength again.

The fire gave a flicker in the grate, bringing me out of my brown study. Time to go and say good-night to Tatiana.

It was shortly after ten, and the night was dark and calm. As I approached the shed, I heard an odd sound—an uncanny grunting that seemed to come from somewhere. I hopped quickly out of the dark and into the shed, switching the light on as I did so.

The noise was coming from Tatiana. She didn't even acknowledge my arrival, which she usually did with a friendly toss of the head, but stood in the corner staring straight ahead of her, her short breaths accompanied by little throaty rasps that indicated that she was in pain.

A thin stab of fear went through me. "Tatiana?"

She didn't even turn around. I went to her side and smoothed the hairy old neck; I wasn't sure if she had a temperature. Then I noticed the odd, stiff way she was standing and—worse than ever—a sunkenness about her eyes.

I turned and leaped from the shed, crossed the yard in a few strides and ran through the house to the telephone. My fingers trembled as I dialed the vet's number. I had read—I forget where—that the sunken eye was the sign of approaching death in cattle.

Hours seemed to pass while the phone rang; at last the vet's wife answered. She was sorry, she told me, but her husband had gone to a difficult calving several miles away. Though she took the message, she didn't sound hopeful.

I went back to the shed, where my Uncle George's old companion stood in a circle of yellow lamplight, a dull, sick look in her eyes. I stroked her neck and talked to her, but she ignored me. After I could stand the appalling grunting sound no longer, I dashed once more out of the shed. I ran along the edge of my field, through a gap in the hawthorn hedge, jumped the ditch and began stumbling up the incline to Beck Farm. There were no lights on.

I hammered on the front door and waited, gasping for breath. Lights appeared and eventually the back door was flung open. He was pulling a dressing gown around him, and when he saw me his face stiffened. I didn't flinch under his icy stare, though.

"What the devil—Joanna! You know I have to be up early for milking—"

"I'm sorry!" I cried, "but, please, help me! It's Tatiana, she's sick—she's dying!"

His expression changed. He planted two great

hands on my shoulders and gave me a vigorous shake. Then he asked if I'd called the vet, and when I told him the details, he said, "Two minutes. Just stand there and take some deep breaths."

He was as good as his word, and soon we were bumping round the rutted track in his Land Rover. We parked in front of my house and hurried into the cowshed. Tatiana was lying down as if it was all too much for her, her grunting more pronounced.

For one who had suggested getting the butcher in, Sam Alderson was a different man. We both knelt, and he palpated her throat very gently and then listened to her breathing; he patted her and spoke to her in wordless, soothing sounds; he asked me a lot of questions about her health, and I was able to answer most of them.

·"Well, there's nothing we can do until the vet gets here," he said at length. "But I don't think it's a throat ulcer, and she's not choking, nor is she in the right condition for mastitis—" He turned on me a reassuring, rather teasing smile.

Whether it was the sight of Tatiana prostrated, the financial worries or the kindness of his tone, I don't know, but my eyes filled with tears. I turned away sharply, and Sam Alderson, for once, seemed to find nothing unusual about his antagonistic neighbor sitting with her back to him and one hand absently stroking her cow's ears. I heard him pull a bale of straw over to support Tatiana's shoulder. Then I felt his warm, strong hand cover mine and hold it, protectively, until the vet arrived.

I might have guessed that Tatiana was not dying. She had swallowed one of my screwdrivers. The vet performed a small operation and removed it.

Later Sam and I gave the vet tea, then saw him on his way. Sam walked through the sitting room with me and stood by the fire.

"I've been meaning to ask you a question..." he began.

"Oh, don't," I said emphatically, slumping in a chair. "Just let me hang on another few months, then I think I'll be forced to sell up, and you can have poor Uncle George's acres and—"

"Wait a minute!" His expression was all confusion. "Is this the girl who braved the elements and won? The girl who scaled rooftops in gales and sank her Italian leather boots in the you-know-what?"

I glanced at him. He was smiling, but not mocking. He was curious. I started telling him about how I could barely hope to make a living by staying here. I told him all my worries, and also that I could never go back to a life of pavements and office blocks. It was a relief to tell someone.

"Now I know," he said at the end, "why old George left this place to you. You must have been the only other person in the family tough enough to take it on. But, you know, it's time you realized something; you've proved your point. Stop hammering yourself into the ground."

I studied his face, puzzled. "But I—"

"Darling, if you'd really rather live here than in a smart town flat—well, I've been hoping you'll say yes to my proposition. How about coming into partnership with me?"

"Partnership?" I asked suspiciously. "You don't mean it, do you?"

He laughed and shook his head. "Joanna. Joanna. Of course I do."

Slowly I began to trust him, began to smile. Then I went into a kind of rapture. "Oh—Sam! It'll mean I can buy a new tractor, and maybe some more cattle, and put a new roof on the chicken run...." I jumped up in excitement, but there he stopped me. He evidently had additional ideas about what a partnership would mean. And suddenly, to my astonishment, I was in full and delicious agreement with him. It was a long, long time before we drew apart and sat down, looking at each other in the firelight.

"Anyway," he said gruffly, "it'll get around the nuisance of your scrounging winter feed from me."

I smiled. "Is that all?"

"No," he said. "I was thinking of something long-term. Does that suit you?"

I meditated on the possibilities. Then I said peacefully, "Yes. Oh, yes."

6 | THE COMMISSION
BY RACHEL MURRAY

What an awful man! What a—a creature! Julie was seething as she replaced the receiver. Who did he think he was, to announce his imminent arrival as if he were royalty, and to say that he intended to watch over his aunt's interests very closely.... What was that supposed to mean?

Anyway, she would soon know; he would be there in half an hour or so. Julie glanced through the front window. Wayne Interiors was at the quiet end of the High Street, but the busy Cotswold village was alive with early tourists and shoppers.

Her senses were as alert as always when a commission was possible. She knew that her quickness, flair and real ability had brought her this far, but each new client was another step along the road to success. Time for a quick flip around the studio before he came, time to cast an eye over the plain, understated and uncompromisingly modern display.

She turned swiftly, her small curvaceous form darting about with surprising speed. She finally uncovered the typewriter for a couple of quick letters before that creature arrived.

As she signed and folded the letters, Julie's deceptively gentle blue eyes gazed down at the desk. She could visualize him quite clearly: small and dark, with horn-rimmed glasses and slicked-down hair; yes, he would have thin lips and clammy hands. A pin-striped suit probably, and a shiny black car big enough for at least eight overweight matrons. His aunt would definitely be an overweight matron with weird ideas on interior decor.

A young woman interrupted this fascinating train of thought, entering through the studio door carrying a chubby, dark-haired baby on her arm. "Julie, do you want to check the green curtains before I give them the final press?"

The Birmingham accent contrasted oddly with her exotic appearance, but at least her name, Yolande, was apt. With Boris, her husband, and the baby, Toby, she rented the connecting cottage and had a working arrangement with Julie. Boris was an artist and Julie sometimes bought his pictures for clients, but the main pivot of the relationship was Yolande's sewing. Her work was beautiful, and she made all the soft furnishings for Wayne Interiors in the little workroom over the studio.

"Carry on, Yolande. I'm sure they'll be super. If you finish them off I'll go and put them up in the morning."

The big, rather battered gray car pulled onto the cobbled forecourt as Yolande went back next door. Julie looked out. Well, well! If this was the bumptious fellow of the phone call, he didn't quite look the part. Tall and slim, with rough-hewn features tanned to a deep gold, he looked more like a successful farmer in his tweed jacket and roll-necked sweater. Julie mentally jettisoned the pinstriped suit and slicked-down hair. This fellow looked quite ordinary and, she might as well admit to herself, equally pleasant.

She met him at the door, quietly composed. "Mr. Boscombe? I'm Julie Wayne."

"Yes, James Boscombe." Gray eyes looked down from what seemed an immense height. "As I explained on the phone, I've called on behalf of my aunt. I'm staying with her for a few days, and as I was in the village this afternoon I said I'd look in on you."

"I see. And what can I do for your aunt?"

"She has this idea of having the whole house done over professionally, every stick of furniture changed. Selling all the old stuff."

Julie's blue eyes looked up into his gray ones. "I have had some experience of that type of conversion," she acknowledged gently.

James Boscombe raised his dark eyebrows. "What do you specialize in, Miss Wayne? That stuff over there?" He waved a large hand at the display.

"Modern decor is my specialty," she admitted, remaining pleasant with difficulty, and feeling the first flush of annoyance steal over her cheeks.

"And do you have any qualifications?"

"My main qualifications are my satisfied clients, but I have a fine arts degree, a diploma in interior design, three years with a reputable firm and two years here on my own."

"Hm. I see. I suppose your charges are pretty high?" He looked down keenly at Julie's pink face.

"Will you be financing this project, Mr. Boscombe?"

"I certainly won't," he replied, and his tone cast a slur on her profession.

"In that case, I'll discuss my charges with your aunt." Her tone was crisp, dismissive.

James Boscombe looked slightly deflated.

"Miss Wayne," he said, "perhaps I should explain that as an architect I have had one or two bad experiences with interior-design firms. I know they often expect money for jam. Believe me, I'm not trying to be objectionable."

"No? Then for someone who isn't trying...." In spite of herself, Julie's voice trembled slightly. This was an awful start; who ever heard of having a slanging match with a prospective customer or, at least, with her nephew? She tried to smile. "I could quite possibly take on a large commission at the moment. I'm not too tied up. But first I must see the house and meet your aunt."

It was a truce of a sort. Each unbent a little. It was agreed that they drive over to Miss Boscombe right away. Julie fixed with Yolande to keep an eye on the studio for casual callers, then jumped into her van to follow James Boscombe to his aunt's house.

The house was small and beautifully proportioned, its mellow golden stone making a graceful contrast to the fresh green of the spring foliage. At first sight Julie felt that this would be a house that cried out for period furniture. Eagerly she walked up the steps, smiling in rueful self-reproof as Hilary Boscombe came out to meet them. She was hardly an overweight matron, but tall and spare, her thin, fine-boned face surrounded by an unruly mass of gray hair.

Introductions over, Julie followed Miss Boscombe into the sitting room. She stopped in her tracks. "You have some lovely pieces here," she said in astonishment. "Have you quite decided to part with all of them?"

"Absolutely. The only thing I'm undecided about is the desk. The rest can go. This house is too cluttered for me. I can't move about, I can't work properly. I am a writer, as my nephew maybe told you. Next week I leave for a lecture tour of the States; I shall be back early in August. Can you do it by then?"

"I should have to know more about what you want done before I could promise that."

"Right. Come and see the other rooms. I want your opinion on changing their use. The kitchen you can leave until the autumn, and the bedrooms. But what do you think of changing over the dining room and the study? I entertain very seldom, on the other hand the study is overflowing with my stuff...."

James stood by as they moved around, his eyes downcast, his expression thoughtful. Julie wished he would clear off and leave them. It made her oddly self-conscious.

In the sitting room Hilary leaned back in an ornate brocade chair. "I have provisionally arranged with Watkins and Jewell to sell the stuff. I've known them both for years; they won't let me down."

James moved in from the door. "I shall drive over from time to time, of course, to see that everything is as Aunt Hilary wants it."

Julie's back stiffened. Miss Boscombe turned to her nephew. "That's all right, James. I shall give Miss Wayne full responsibility. If she pleased Mona Benson, she'll please me. She's got sense."

Julie allowed herself a faint curve of the lips. Her professional integrity was as dear to her as her life's blood. She would refuse a commission rather than commit herself to work that displeased her. She turned to Miss Boscombe. "Before we go any further, I must know what you have in mind to replace your furnishings."

"Modern," was the decisive reply. "Modern. Plain. Good. Uncluttered. Expensive if necessary. No wobbly tables. No bobbles and tassels. And it must feel good. I like things to be right when I touch them."

Julie relaxed slightly. "Your house will take it," she said, "though I had my doubts as we came up the drive. It will need a great deal of care—"

"Which will no doubt necessitate a great deal of expense," interrupted James.

He didn't miss a trick, did he? "Have you changed your mind about financing the project, Mr. Boscombe?"

"No, but I've heard that line used before." He nodded coolly and strolled into the hall.

Julie breathed deeply and turned to Hilary again. "I need at least a couple of hours with you before I can even do preliminary sketches."

"That's sensible. It will have to be after seven-thirty today; I have someone here till then, and tomorrow I go away for the weekend."

Julie suggested that she return at seven forty-five, and they agreed on this.

"Just a minute, though," said Hilary. "Why go back twenty miles or so? James could take you for a meal."

"No, thank you, Miss Boscombe," said Julie briskly. "I have a few things to see to. I'll come back as we arranged."

Calmly she walked past James and went out to the van. Was it her imagination or had he stretched out a hand as she passed, as if to detain her?

She drove back through the sun-dappled lanes feeling strung out. This would be her biggest job so far, especially if she did the whole house. It must be good. She would show that creature. She would make it the highlight of the last two years. Her single-minded dedication to her career was a little unusual, she knew. No men friends cluttered her life. Of course there had been the odd casual relationship, but nothing had interfered with her work. Vaguely she acknowledged that she might someday find someone to love more than she loved her work, and then her life would have to change, but not yet—oh no, certainly not yet.

As she turned into the High Street the ambulance on the little forecourt looked alien and businesslike. What on earth...?

She leaped out of the van and ran across to the next-door cottage.

"Thank heaven you're back," gasped Yolande, gripping Julie's arm and dragging her inside. "It's Boris. He's broken his shoulder or collarbone or something and hurt his leg. He was up in that tree again; you know, I told you he's been up there lately doing sketches of the river." Tears glistened in Yolande's incredibly beautiful eyes. "I knew it would end in trouble; he's not the agile type. I must go with him to the hospital, and it's almost Toby's bedtime. Could you bathe him like you did before? His supper is in the kitchen."

Julie looked at her friend and thought not of her appointment with Miss Boscombe but, strangely, of the little blue-and-white bedroom with the yellow ducks on the rug and a fat cuddly teddy waiting in the cot. She gave Yolande a quick hug. "Don't worry. I'll see to him, and I'll be here till you get back."

Inside the cottage Toby was in his playpen, standing cockily on one leg, clutching the bars with damp, sticky fingers.

Julie went to the phone and explained the situation to Miss Boscombe. "Don't worry, Miss Wayne; if you will have finished with the little boy by about eight, James will bring me over then."

"That's fine," she said thankfully. "I'm so sorry to put you to the trouble, but I must stay with him."

As she lifted Toby out of the playpen, Julie felt once again that strange tightening of the heart. His small body was so warm. It was soft, yet sturdy and solid. A little boy. What would it be like to have a little boy of her own? She pulled herself up abruptly. It made her a bit soft when she was dealing with Toby.

The time flew past as she painstakingly bathed the baby. It took ages because it was only the second time that she had given him his supper and put him to bed on her own. He looked at her seriously with his huge dark eyes as he drank his milk and had his six teeth brushed with the tiny soft toothbrush.

In his cot he looked around alertly and was already standing up as Julie left the room. She hurried through the sewing room back to her flat, leaving the doors open so that she could listen for him.

Quick, get out the coffee set, whip around with the duster. Tidy yourself up and change. Issuing instructions to herself, she washed and changed into black velvet trousers and a pale pink sweater. She was brushing her hair when the ball rang.

As she ushered her guests into the flat Julie knew a swift satisfaction that they were seeing it at its best. The low evening sun glowed through the big window at the back, filling the long room with a soft light and picking out the jewel tones of the rugs.

"What a lovely room, my dear," said Hilary. "Isn't it splendid, James?"

"It's beautiful," agreed James quietly, turning to Julie. "It suits you perfectly."

Good grief, she thought, *he's human. That was a very nicely turned compliment.* She smiled her thanks at him.

They had coffee and then she settled down with samples, photographs and her notebook, ready for a searching analysis of her client's likes and dislikes. Before the first question was out of her mouth, an agonized wail came from Toby next door. "I'm so sorry," she said, "I won't be a minute; he's missing his mommy."

She let down the side of Toby's cot. Louder wails filled the room when he saw it was Julie and not Yolande. No amount of soothing and petting would pacify him. Reluctantly, she wrapped him in a blanket and took him back to her visitors. "I'm afraid I can't leave him," she said. "I'll let him play on the floor until his mommy comes back."

"I'll look after him," said James unexpectedly. "You carry on with Aunt Hilary."

Julie looked up in relief as he took Toby from her. He smiled at the baby, the first smile she had seen on his face. It was astonishingly attractive. Toby stuck out his jaw and showed his teeth, smiling back with all his considerable charm. He was quite ready to play.

After half an hour Julie felt that she was beginning to see what Hilary wanted, finding what she needed and how much she was prepared to spend.

She learned that the reason for the change was that Hilary's sister had died three months before, after keeping house for them both in the family home. After a lifetime of weaving her way around little tables and spindly chairs, Hilary wanted something different. Plain, new, solid. Julie's heart lifted.

By ten o'clock Toby had been returned to his relieved mother, with good news of Boris, and Julie was satisfied that she had a good grounding for the job.

"I will let you have sketches, samples of materials and an estimate of my charges early next week," she said, as she showed her guests out.

Hilary was pleased. "A sensible girl," she was saying to James as they went to the car. "Sensible" was apparently her highest form of praise.

Going back upstairs after locking up for the night, Julie felt fatigue for the first time that day. *Seven hours ago I hadn't heard of the Boscombes*, she thought. *I'll show him. I'll show him that Wayne Interiors is good.*

Julie left Watkins and Jewell's auction rooms with mixed feelings. She had followed her instincts and bought back the huge mahogany desk that Harriet had finally decreed must go. *I'm mad*, she thought, *I really am.*

She had felt that it was a painful parting for Hilary when the desk went, and she had resolved to plan the study with the desk as the focal point.

The weeks flew past with Julie at the center of organized chaos, as walls were stripped down, decorating started and new furniture stored temporarily in bedrooms. There were visits to London, phone calls to suppliers, accessories to search for.

It was a relief to be able to rely on her usual men for the painting and decorating. Elderly brothers, Jacob and Jonathan were good workers and had a relationship with Julie of mutual respect and admiration.

By mid-July things were going well. The sitting room was almost finished. In accordance with Hilary's wishes, it was above all a peaceful, relaxing room. Subdued oatmeals and caramel colors with, still to come, highlights of peacock and gold. Julie looked at it and knew it was good.

The new dining room also was going well, the decorations nearly finished, carpeting ready to lay, curtains ready to hang. Furniture was ordered but, as often happened, had not yet arrived.

The study would be the last room to be completed.

Contrary to her expectations there had been no interference from James Boscombe. She had seen him only once since the evening at her flat. A few weeks earlier he had called at the house and found Julie in her dungarees, ripping out the old bookshelves. He was polite and attentive as she pointed out what was scheduled to be done next, but said very little, and after reminding Julie to contact him if necessary, he left as suddenly as he had appeared.

She stood there afterward, covered in dust, baggy dungarees pulled in around her tiny waist with an ancient leather belt, wondering why she felt disappointed. Was it because she had expected a verbal sparring match again, or was it because she had hoped for some approval of her efforts?

Suddenly the room seemed stifling. Dust was everywhere. The day was oppressively hot, with hardly a breath of air. She sat on the floor, her back to the wall, and felt that it was all too much. Why was she flogging herself at such a rate? She had been living on quick snack meals, working till all hours.

The knowledge lay deep within her that it could be because of James. She had to prove to him that Wayne Interiors was not a firm that expected "money for jam." She had been determined that he be made to eat his words, and all at once it seemed an empty plan. He had been today for the first time and had left within ten minutes, after showing the minimum of interest in what she was doing. Julie bent her tousled head and rested it on her knees.

Suddenly footsteps sounded on the bare boards of the hall. James had returned and stood, cool and immaculate, in the doorway, eyes looking startlingly gray against his deep tan.

"I almost forgot to ask after Toby," he said. "How is—are you all right, Julie?" Stooping, he grasped her hands and without more ado pulled her to her feet and out through the French windows to the terrace.

"What on earth's wrong with you, girl, stifling yourself in that dusty hole? Get some fresh air into your lungs, for goodness' sake." He pushed her down onto the low wall.

She looked up at him in astonishment. Good heavens, it was impossible to weigh him up. One minute he treated her like a piece of furniture, the next like a Victorian miss with the vapors.

"Don't worry about me. I'm quite all right," she said edgily. "It's just the heat."

"I'm not worried about you—not at all. But it's insane to be inside in that heat and dust when you could be out here in the fresh air."

Anger flared in Julie. "I have a job to do and a living to earn. I wouldn't manage either if I spent all my time lounging in the garden every time the sun shone!"

They glared at each other in silence. Then James shrugged his shoulders and turned to go. He handed her a small parcel. "I forgot—I thought this might amuse Toby. Will you give it to him for me, please?" He turned away and was gone, leaving Julie sitting there feeling completely drained of all energy and initiative. *He called me Julie,* she thought in dull surprise.

That had been weeks ago. Since then she had taken herself in hand, eaten properly, made sure of enough sleep and left all heavy moving to the Jarvis brothers. She told herself that everything had been getting out of perspective. She would do her best work for Hilary, as for any other client. All the extra effort, the late-night work, must stop.

Yolande was proving an immense help. All the curtains were beautifully made, as usual, and she had even turned her hand to creating a shaggy deep-pile rug when Julie had been unable to find one in the right shade of gold.

Toby was trying to walk by himself, and had four more teeth. His present from James was a great success. It was a diesel train in smoothly polished wood, which let out a piercingly authentic two-tone note when it was pushed along. His taking it to bed with him and cuddling it instead of his teddy was a mark of the highest possible favor.

Hilary was due back by mid-August, and in the third week of July Jonathan was incapacitated by a strained knee. Jacob delivered a prepared and stilted speech to Julie saying that, though he understood her difficulties, she must find someone else to do the study—he couldn't possibly tackle it without Jonathan.

Afterward, in spite of her dismay, Julie smiled to herself. She thought of them as the Siamese twins, one half totally incapable of appearing for work without the other.

But time was pressing. She resolved to do the study walls and ceiling herself. Quite used to hard physical work, she ran up and down the ladder with an energy born of urgency. The ceiling was to be pale turquoise, the walls white. Fortunately the bookshelves were freestanding, the plainest she could find in a wood similar to the desk, which of course was the most important piece in the whole room.

With two days to go before Hilary's return, the study was finished. Julie knew the deep satisfaction of the creative artist at the end of a job well done. Now for the books, stored in boxes in a bedroom.

It was a hot, drowsy Saturday afternoon. The church bells down in the village were ringing for a wedding, sounding joyous and lively in contrast to the quiet of the house. It was impossible to move the boxes full of books. All right, so she would carry a pile at a time downstairs until the whole lot was in order on the shelves.

At teatime she boiled an egg and cut bread and butter in the kitchen, ready to spend all the evening, if necessary, toiling with the books. Her thin summer dress was sticking damply to her back, and she was nowhere near finished. The curved outline of the long chair at the back of the room seemed seductively inviting, its pale leather soft and cool. She would rest for a few minutes. But at once she fell into the deep, dreamless sleep of exhaustion.

She awoke slowly, opening her eyes to the soft glow of the lamps. What time was it? It was quite dark outside. Who had lit the lamps? She slid off the chair. The bookshelves were full. She glanced at her watch.

"It's about then," said a deep voice from the hall. James was there, carrying out the empty book boxes. "Did I startle you? I'm sorry. I felt a little like the prince when he saw Sleeping Beauty, but I thought I had better not do what he did, and awaken you with a kiss." He smiled. "The books are finished; there's no more work for you today."

Julie smiled at him in gratitude, then suddenly her heart began to thump heavily, painfully. *Sleeping Beauty! Waken me with a kiss!* She blushed bright pink. Why on earth did she always feel so on edge when she was with him? She felt her bare feet sink into the soft pile of the hall carpet and realized she must look a complete wreck. Crumpled dress, bare legs; goodness only knew what her hair and face were like.

"I must go up and change," she said. "I keep these old clothes here to work in."

"Don't be long," he said, and then, incredibly, "I have some supper ready for you."

After a wash, she changed quickly back into the yellow pleated skirt and sleeveless top she had worn when coming over. That was better. Why did she always have to look so ghastly when James appeared on the scene?

They had supper in the kitchen. He had prepared a mixed salad with cheese, followed by peaches and dark strong coffee. He was kind, he was gentle, teasing her about all her journeys up and down stairs with the books. Julie looked at him as he poured her coffee. Where was that creature she had so wanted to impress?

When they had finished she asked if he would like to see over the rooms, and together they left the kitchen. He was very quiet as she switched on lights, drew curtains and explained her reasons for certain colors or effects. Why was he so quiet? Didn't he like it? Very hesitantly she went before him into the study. James went over to the desk and looked at her questioningly.

She flushed. He must have thought she was crazy. "I just felt I had to get it back from Watkins and Jewell," she said hurriedly. "I had this feeling that your aunt wanted to keep it, so, well, here it is."

"I had a letter yesterday from Aunt Hilary," he said. "She's looking forward so much to seeing what you've done. She says only thing worries her: letting the old desk go. She's frightened she won't work well without it!"

Speechlessly Julie looked at him. Two fat teardrops slid down her cheeks. What an end to the day!

James took her hand. His face was set. "Julie," he said. "Julie." He saw the tears. "You're tired out! Come on, I'll drive you home."

Too overcome to argue, Julie took her seat by his side in the car. In a small voice, she asked, "Did you like it? The house, I mean."

"It's absolutely wonderful, Julie," he said. "It's completely right for Aunt Hilary. It left me quite speechless with admiration." There was a silence of several minutes. "Julie," he said again, "I want to apologize for being·so impossible when we first met. I thought you were one of these money-grabbing females, dead set on a career and hard as hell."

She said slowly, "You were right about the career part of it. What changed your mind about me?"

"Seeing you with young Toby," he said. "I soon realized I was way off the mark, and I knew myself for the world's biggest fool. I have been wanting to come over to apologize for ages, but I felt so awful and, well, I didn't think you wanted me around."

They drew up outside the studio. "Oh, but I did," she protested. "That day when I was ripping out the bookshelves, I felt so let down when you only stayed for a few minutes, and then we ended up so cross with each other."

James stared at her, his face in shadow. "We have a lot to sort out, Julie. Go to bed now—you've had quite a day. I'll come around in the morning. Good night; sleep well."

"Good night and...thank you, James."

She went up to her flat in a daze. He liked her. He had liked her all the time. All those weeks when she had been planning to make him grovel, and she had been so miserable. And now the world was suddenly a lovely place because he liked her.

The morning was cool and sunny. Julie was up early, and after breakfast went out to cut flowers ready to arrange in the studio. She could keep an eye on the street from in there.

Toby came out with Boris for his morning walk, wearing his new red shoes. He would go for a long way holding just one finger of his daddy's hand, but sat down with a bump after seven or eight steps on his own. They waved to Julie as they passed. She blew Toby a kiss.

They were coming back again when James arrived and tooted his horn at them.

He joined Julie in the garden and they had a little inconsequential conversation about gardening. Then suddenly he said, "Julie, how do you feel about taking on another commission?"

Blankly, she stared at him. She hadn't expected this. "I—I can't," she stammered. "Your aunt...."

He took both her hands and looked down at her, his eyes dark and anxious. "I mean a permanent commission, as my wife!"

Time stood still. The church bells pealed exuberantly. Then the two figures merged in an embrace.

7 LIFE IS FOR LIVING
BY JO FRANCIS

Maria stepped off the London train and walked quickly along the deserted platform. She felt suddenly lost and alone: a feeling of overwhelming strangeness enveloped her, and she wished she had not made the journey to Stateley-on-Sea.

She didn't quite know why she had come. The trauma of Robert's desertion six months before had engendered a longing for the old safe times of her childhood. After the rows and bitter recrimination that had taken place when her parents had learned of her affair, she had not been back to Stateley. "I'll live my own life," she had stormed. "You don't understand. I'm young. Life is for living!"

"There will always be a welcome here for you," her mother had replied sadly, and she had meant it. Maria knew that, but she had not been back. She could not have done so, for there would have been no welcome for Robert.

Now, on a sudden impulse, Maria had returned. She was standing alone on the platform at Stateley. The clean crisp air of the coastal town was all about her. She had not written to her parents to tell them of her intention. She did not know how to make the first move toward a reconciliation, for her mother had been right: Robert had left her.

The station itself had changed from the days of her childhood and even from the days of her visits home from college. The old green paint had been peeling then. Now the building gleamed fresh white, which endowed it with an alien, almost foreign, atmosphere.

Five years ago Mrs. Mitchell would have waved to her from behind the security of the bookstall. There would have been a welcoming smile on the lined face of old Jack at the ticket barrier or a saucy remark from young Mike as she was swept into Tom's strong arms. She did not want to remember Tom. She had not thought of him for years. There had been no room for him in her life in London. There had been no room for anyone except Robert.

Today there was nothing. Her face meant nothing to the lean-faced man holding out his hand for her ticket.

The row of taxis stood sentinel in the yard before the station entrance, for even out of the summer season people took a few days' holiday in the bracing sea air of the small town. Maria wrinkled her nose appreciatively. The wind was blowing off the sea and bringing with it the pungent odor of salt and seaweed and fish from the vicinity of the quay. She tucked the fur collar of her coat comfortingly around her ears as she felt the rough caress of the salt wind on her face.

Stateley was a flat and windy place, a place frequented by the yachting fraternity and by countless families with small children who loved to dig on the sandy beach that stretched so invitingly and safely along the coast. It was a place for jeans and flat shoes.

The taxi driver took her small case. She was aware that the man eyed her curiously. She smiled inwardly; once—long ago—she had looked at a citified stranger in that way.

"Beechcroft Hotel," she said.

"Are you staying long?"

"Just a week."

The friendly voice invited her confidence; his eyes in the rearview mirror reminded her disconcertingly of Tom's. "I lived here as a child," she added. "Down by the quay. My father was the lifeboat engineer and we lived above the boathouse. He's retired now."

"Like to see it?" He smiled into the mirror, and without waiting for her reply, he turned the taxi sharply and headed toward the long esplanade and the sea. He reached a brown hand across the cab as if he had read her unspoken thoughts and turned the switch on the meter. "No extra charge," he murmured softly as she frowned. She could not see his face, but she wished the eyes in the mirror did not remind her of the boy she had known.

Tom Sands had been in her life all the days of her childhood. Her first memory of him had been as a small boy of eight curled up asleep in the hidden darkness of the lifeboat. When he shut up the lifeboat house for the night her father had found Tom. He had lifted the boy out of the boat and carried him in his strong arms to the flat above. Her mother had made hot soup, and Tom had dunked great chunks of fresh bread in it while the tears welled in his large gray eyes.

Maria had twisted her dark pigtail thoughtfully in her small hands and stared at the boy.

"Why were you sleeping in the boat?" she demanded.

"Hush, dear," whispered her mother. "Tom was just resting."

"But he shouldn't have been in the boat," insisted Maria. "Daddy never lets us get in the boat." She pointed a finger accusingly at Tom. "Were you running away?" Her voice took on a shrill, excited quality as her quick mind embraced the magnitude of possible reasons for such an enterprise.

"I was pretending there was a wreck on Foxborough Head and I was going to rescue the sailors," the boy said falteringly. "I must go home now. My mom will be waiting tea."

He stood up. He didn't look like a child at all. He looked like a small man. It was something to do with the way he stood, stocky and firm in his rubber boots. Maria's father put a hand on his shoulder in a man-to-man gesture that shut her out.

"Come and see me again; I'll show you the lifeboat," he offered.

Tom came...and came again. He helped polish the brass plaques recording the rescues of shipwrecked sailors by the Stateley lifeboat, while Maria sat curled up on the coiled rope and listened to their men's talk. He spent all the hours of daylight he could along the beach. As soon as he was old enough he worked every Saturday morning at the yacht center.

He still spent time in the lifeboat house and teased Maria and was her best friend. He watched as she gathered a crowd of teenagers around her, but he did not join the group. While Maria was studying for her examinations and enjoying discos and sailing, he was working as an engineering apprentice at the boatyard. He grew stocky and strong; his sturdy stance became more pronounced... and Maria could not imagine life without him.

One summer evening she walked across the slipway and leaned her arms on the railing of the long esplanade. The sun was golden, low in the sky, when she felt his quiet presence beside her.

"What now, Maria?" he asked softly. "No disco? No party?" And she knew instinctively that he was smiling in the dusk.

"Not tonight."

"Then we'll walk to Foxborough Head," he announced firmly. He took her hand in his, and his touch sent a strange tingling response running up and down her arm.

The night was warm as they strolled along the soft sand and climbed the rough path to the headland. The lighthouse beamed its warning across the darkness of the sky and the water as they sat on the worn stone of the old disused quay. Once the quay had been a busy bustling place of trade and sea activity. The old stone customs building was still standing, though its windows were boarded up and it had a sad and desolate air about it. It was long and low, the uneven stones of its walls seeming a part of its rocky surroundings.

Maria dangled her feet above the gently lapping water and felt the quivering of Tom's young body as he leaned against her in the darkness. He took her small hand and held it tightly in his own broad fingers as he bent his face to hers. He kissed her slowly, and Maria wondered at his gentle touch and felt both safe and trapped in the warmth of his arms. He kissed her again as the light from the beam struck the water, and Maria was afraid.

"Wait for me," he murmured softly into the moving strands of her dark hair. She laughed and twisted a piece of hair through her fingers and played with it and smiled up at him...and pretended she had not seen the longing in his eyes.

"For ever and ever," she teased.

"I mean it," he said seriously. "You will go to college, but I shall stay here in Stateley...and I will be waiting for you, Maria."

"I cannot promise," she said levelly, but her generous mouth curled happily and enticingly as she said it. "The world is waiting for me, too. I want to live...." She hesitated and laughed huskily in the dark and added to herself, *a little dangerously*.

"You will come back to me," he said with firm conviction.

Foxborough Head was a dim misty outline against the sea when the taxi turned at the end of the esplanade by the long low building of the beach café. Maria turned to watch it out of sight; she had spent the happy summer there, serving endless burgers and chips, sausages and chips, eggs and chips. She had scooped out ice cream after ice cream for tanned youngsters with sand in their hair. And when the day was over she had climbed the headland with her hand in Tom's. Sometimes they had taken the small dinghy and rowed far out in the calm water beyond the beach and talked of their hopes for the future.

"I'll have a boatyard of my own one day," said Tom.

Maria listened and smiled, but she dreamed of a glittering future for herself among the bright lights of London.

Their happy carefree summer came to an end. Maria went to college and when she came home during the vacations, the broad familiar figure of Tom was waiting. But very soon that part of her life was over.

The bright shining dream of the future was in her eyes and the soft sand of Stateley was still clinging to her feet, but life had begun. She was nineteen. She had a job in the merchandising control section of a large department store in London, and she shared a small flat with three other girls beside the lapping water of the Thames.

She wrote to Tom and he answered belatedly in a large and stilted hand... and his letters seemed almost to come from a stranger. The silent strength of his person was not conveyed in the untidy writing. The time that elapsed between their letters grew longer, until the intimacy of their youth had faded.

Within a few months of her arrival she met Robert at the launch of a big sales promotion at the store. Her dream was no longer a dream but a reality. She lived at a bustling, rushing pace as Robert pursued her with single-minded determination. She had no time to think. He sent presents of flowers and chocolates with the ease and charm of a successful man... and Robert was successful in any project he undertook.

He undertook the conquest of Maria... and she was fascinated and flattered by his attention and thought herself in love. She did not believe the gossip of her colleagues. She did not believe her mother who told her bluntly, "He's a philanderer, my dear. He will leave you when he has won your love."

She left the small flat by the river and moved alone to a more comfortable one... and Robert was a frequent visitor.

In the beginning Maria hoped—almost expected—that Robert would ask her to marry him. Three years after their meeting he had not done so, and she watched helplessly as their relationship began to lose its excitement for him. She guessed that he had met another girl, but she dared not ask him.

She could see the pity in the eyes of his friends. She knew they were saying among themselves, "He's tired of Maria. She's trying too hard."

She felt as soon as she opened the door of the flat on that dreadful day that something was wrong. It wasn't only the silence of the empty flat as she walked in. Robert's coat was not on the hook in the small hall. She went into the kitchen and felt the same desolate emptiness around her.

The new camera he had recently bought her lay on the bed where she had left it in the morning. Beside it was a small card; she picked it up with faltering hand and read the words, "Thanks, Ma.   in his neat handwriting. Maria stood and stared at the small white object in her hand. She did not want to understand the meaning of the cryptic note. She did not want to believe that he had left her.

The wasted love of the past years flashed through her mind as she repeated the two words aloud. She ran to the window in a frenzy of despair and opened it and threw the camera out. She laughed as she heard it crash on the hard stone pavement below. It was the last present he had bought her, and it was of no value to her now.

She went on laughing alone in the flat until the

unreal laughter turned to sobs and she slept exhausted on the soft bed.

Now it was over and Maria had come back to the sea. She walked along the one street of shops that was Stateley High Street and marveled at the friendly chatter around her, for the summer season was over, and the women with their shopping baskets and children in tow were not strangers to one another as were the shoppers in the crowded streets around her own small flat. She bought herself a pair of blue jeans and some sweaters and went back to the hotel and tied her hair in a rough pony tail. Then she ran down to the beach to the row of dinghies parked along the sand. The boatman was a young student, his face and arms well burned by the recent summer sun. He looked doubtfully at her well-manicured hands as she paid for the rental of a dinghy.

"Are you sure you can handle it?" he asked.

"I've been used to the sea all my life," Maria retorted sharply, and she rowed the boat firmly away from the shore toward the gray-green outline of Foxborough Head.

Half an hour later she reached the rocks by the lighthouse, and she turned the boat and rowed steadily into the old quay beneath the headland. She tied up the dinghy to one of the old mooring rings and looked around her. The crumbling wall where she had sat with Tom had been rebuilt, and several boats were moored there. The old stone customs house building had been roofed, and a gleam of sunshine glinted on its glass windows. A large yacht was docked in the slipway.

A man and a boy seated on a plank slung alongside the yacht were rhythmically painting the hull a glowing red. The man was stocky and the swing of his arm was powerful and steady.

Maria clambered slowly up the iron stepladder on the wall of the quay. The stiffness in her legs was almost painful, and she rubbed her thighs with her small hands. Leaning on the stone parapet, she felt the warmth of the sun on her back as she watched the two painters working on the hull of the yacht. They moved gradually along the plank until they reached its end, and the man climbed lithely onto the deck of the yacht. Maria smiled. She had forgotten the sure-footed stance of a man of the sea.

He crossed the deck and jumped to the land. He looked at Maria and a smile wreathed his face and reached his gray eyes, and her heart beat suddenly faster at the recognition on his face. She had seen that smile a long, long time ago.

"So you've come home at last," he said.

"Just a short visit."

"I heard you were living in London."

"Yes. . . . You're still working on boats," she remarked in the old teasing way.

He laughed with the hidden smile of the boy. Then he walked unhurriedly to the long stone building and placed the paint pots inside the door and the brushes in a jar. Maria followed and stood silently beside him. pulled the great doors partly shut and the white ring showed starkly bright against the dark green surface: TOM SANDS. Boatyard.

He glanced at the mark on her finger where she had worn Robert's ring. Then he looked away, toward the lighthouse on the rocks and far out to the distant horizon.

"I'm brewing up a pot of tea. Would you like some?"

"Please."

She stood beside him as he filled the kettle and plugged it into the new socket on the old stone wall. She smelled the oiled wool of his seamen's jersey. It was the familiar smell of her father's clothing during the days of her childhood. He poured the tea carefully into two large mugs and carried them over to the wall, and they sat upon the edge of the quay. Their feet dangled over the edge as they had when the couple played there as children; as they had on the day Tom first kissed Maria.

She laughed as she saw the wobbling reflection of their legs in the moving water beneath them.

"Why didn't you come back?" he asked quietly, as the sun turned the sky into a beautiful tapestry of blue and gray and pink.

"I don't know. Perhaps it was because I became a Londoner." Her high-pitched tinkling laugh grated on her ears. His eyes were boring into hers.

"What else?" he demanded.

"There was a man," she added recklessly. "A man I could not bring home to Stateley...so I did not come myself."

He did not say anything. He slowly sipped the tea from the mug in his hand and watched the changing colors of the sky. She felt the warmth of his jersey against her arm, and she did not mind the silence that had come between them. She felt no compulsion to fill the void with idle words as she would have done if Robert had been beside her. She threw a fallen crust of bread to a circling gull. It swooped toward them and caught her offering in midair and flew away.

The waves of the sea were beckoning Maria as they had so many years ago. She was sure that Tom knew of her life with Robert, and she wished that he did not. He pulled her to her feet with his broad strong hands, and he was smiling in the dusk.

"We will go to your home now," he said firmly... and Maria let her hand rest happily in his.

8 | WAITING FOR GRIZELDA
BY ROMA GROVER

If I tell you that I failed to catch John's second name because we were introduced on Victoria Station, I'm sure you will know what I mean. Introductions on railway stations are always cut off in their prime. A guard clangs a door, or a woolly voice announces that the train now standing at Platform Two had been there since 1911. And you are left, as I was, gazing into gorgeous steady gray eyes, not knowing the name of their owner. Except that it was John, and he appeared to be one of Grizelda's entourage.

Apart from that, I knew only that we had converged, he from one side of the station, I from the other, to see my friend Grizelda off on a world tour, though first she had to get to Gatwick to meet her great-aunt. We wished her "bon voyage" and "God speed," bade her take care, enjoy herself, write often. I told her not to worry about a thing but to leave everything to me, and also to make sure she loaded all her luggage on the train, including that awful ukulele she insisted on taking with her.

"Not the ukulele," I recalled saying a week ago, when we were in our bedroom selecting the items Grizelda would need to escort her great-aunt Grizelda, after whom she was named, on a world tour. Grizelda and I had worked together for two years but shared a flat for only two weeks. Her habit of practicing the ukulele far into the night had come as a big surprise. Perhaps shock would be a better word.

"Certainly I must take it," Grizelda said, and giggled. "I shall accompany my aunt on the ukulele. Besides, it will come in handy, I expect."

Instantly I had a mental image of Grizelda gliding along the Amazon, paddling her own canoe with the ukulele; of Grizelda foiling bandits in the Hindu Kush with the ukulele; of Grizelda adding zest to a Spanish Gypsy campfire with her ukulele. I saw firelight gleaming on her face and long fair hair, her Gypsy skirt swirling. Oh yes, Grizelda had style.

"I mean, Harriet, I might even play the thing," she added. "Those sultry tropical nights aren't going to be much fun with only Great-aunt Grizelda for company. You know how Victorian she is." Grizelda flopped down on her bed and ran fingers through her hair. "You know, I really shouldn't be going. There's so much to do here. I mean, I've only just moved in."

"Nonsense," I remember saying. "You must go. It isn't every day you get an invitation like this. Leave everything to me."

I was feeling noble at the time. "I'll even visit Aunt Mildred for you."

Grizelda had two great-aunts: Aunt Grizelda, already mentioned, and Aunt Mildred, who lived round the corner. Grizelda went to visit Mildred every Friday evening, and on the last two Fridays I had gone with her.

"Will you?" Grizelda asked, brightening. "Honestly?"

"Of course," I said. "Just leave it to me."

My newfound nobility didn't last. Instant nobility seldom does. During the following week most of it dwindled, to be replaced by secret envy, but a remnant remained to sustain the wait on the station platform with Grizelda and her luggage and her anonymous friend John. Especially John. I'd sneaked a glance at him once or twice. Several other friends joined us. When the train pulled in, we talked and waved and bestowed many kisses on Grizelda and a great deal of good advice, and then we closed the door and relinquished her to the world. Feeling the loss of departure, we moved away. Suddenly John was beside me.

"Coming my way?" He smiled, and the inflection of his voice shaped ordinary words to an invitation, a special invitation, even though we both knew there was only one way to go. Out through the gate marked Exit.

"Yes," I said, going weak at the knees because of his closeness, his voice, the bit of stray hair that fell over his forehead. Because of everything about him, I suppose. His presence. We walked comfortably together, the way you do sometimes with a stranger, as if we had known each other for years.

Outside the station, London was filled with summer, and beautiful. Bright sunlight honed the chrome of cars caught in a traffic jam. The pavement felt warm beneath the feet. Geraniums bloomed bravely in window boxes, and you knew that come the evening there would be a red sunset staining the Thames. Suddenly I no longer envied Grizelda. London was a good place to be on a summer's day, but perhaps I am not the best judge of that because being with John made me lyrical.

"A cup of coffee?" he asked.

I was supposed to return immediately to the office. Also, there was shopping to be done. Without hesitation I said "Yes," and we went into a coffee place and sat opposite each other and talked about Grizelda and ukuleles.

"I'm glad she took it with her," he said.

"You are?"

"You sound surprised. It's a beautiful instrument," he replied, "though not easy to play. George Formby used to play one."

"I know," I nodded. "But he could. Have you ever spent every evening listening to someone play the ukulele who can't?"

"Yes," he said.

Afraid he might think I was criticizing Grizelda, which, of course, I was not, only her ukulele, I said quickly, "Well, it takes time, I expect."

At the mention of the word "time," he glanced at his watch and I glanced at mine and we both rose and said we must rush. Outside on the street corner, he touched my hand—a gentle, different touch—and said, "May I call and see you one evening next week?"

"Oh yes, please," I replied, and then more calmly, "You'll be very welcome."

"Thank you," he said gravely, and went.

I remained standing on the corner, wondering why I had allowed the only man in the world for me to disappear in the midday crowds without even knowing his name. Who was he and what part did he play in Grizelda's life? He had given her a chaste kiss on the cheek when she left, so it couldn't be a big part. Therefore, could he be safely included among the items she was leaving to me for the next months? Along with Aunt Milly and Grizelda's correspondence and tidying the bedroom, which still bore the signs of departure when I got home that evening.

Grizelda was very untidy. I had discovered that in the past two weeks. Tights sprawled in leaping emptiness across chairs. Eye makeup smeared the dressing table, and already I was missing Grizelda. The last shreds of nobility were quenched by silence as I picked up two deflated dresses from the floor and opened the wardrobe door. Empty coat hangers rattled together, and a wisp of Grizelda's perfume came to meet me, like a ghost. And then I settled down to wait for her letters. And for John.

John didn't arrive, but a card came from Grizelda a few days later, sent from Naples. She was worn out, she said. Absolutely exhausted from trying to keep up with Great-aunt Grizelda. They had whizzed round Rome and Naples, gathering culture and blistered feet, and at the end of each day Aunt Grizelda was still game for a nightclub or two.

The doorbell rang while I was reading the card, and for one absurd moment I thought it might be John, so I made the hair-tidying, pinafore-smoothing gestures women always make even when they are wearing jeans and a bandanna, and opened the door. It was not John. It was an attractive foreign-looking man, and he also seemed to be one of Grizelda's. He was tall, intense, gray suited and he flourished a letter bearing Grizelda's handwriting.

"Grizelda? She is 'ere? What is zis about 'er going round ze world? I will speak wiz 'er." He really did talk like that.

"I'm afraid she's already gone," I said.

"Zen I wait." He came in and sat on our old settee, giving a touch of style to its battered springs and threadbare upholstery. We'd have to do something about that settee.

"She won't be back for another three months at least," I said. "Would you like a cup of tea?"

"Tea? You speak of tea when my Grizelda, she is gone." He waved his arms in an attitude of dejection. "Not 'ere," he repeated sadly. "We were to be engaged, and now.... Tell me, 'ave you ever seen 'er dance wiz bare feets in ze park?" His eyes made a direct appeal.

"No." I didn't know Grizelda did that sort of thing. But I was beginning to realize there were many things I didn't know about Grizelda. She had never mentioned Pierre—that was his name—for one thing. It occurred to me, jubilantly, that if she intended to become engaged to Pierre, then she couldn't be engaged to John at the same time. Or could she?

"I tell you," Pierre went on. "She looked beautiful. And, yes, I will 'ave tea."

I made tea and carried the tray to the living room and sat beside him on the settee. It soon became apparent that his idea of waiting for Grizelda was quite different from mine. Mine meant having a nice little chat about Grizelda and their wedding plans and how they met and where they were going to live and that kind of thing. Pierre's idea included turning down the lights, listening to a Demis Roussos record playing softly and sitting so close I couldn't raise my tea cup.

"You are beautiful too, but in a different way." He quickly shed his air of devastation. "Your leeps," he mused. "Your eyes. The way zat scarf is tied around your 'air. You are ze quiet one, ze domesticated one who would make a man very 'appy."

Inheriting Grizelda's life brought its problems. "Excuse me," I said. "But you can't wait for Grizelda on this settee. It's too uncomfortable."

"Yes," he agreed. "It is."

I jumped up.

"A spring 'as 'it you?" he inquired lazily.

"Not yet," I said. "Look, I'm sorry, Pierre, but you must go and wait for Grizelda somewhere else."

He raised a very quizzical, very French eyebrow. "You do not like me?"

"Oh, it isn't that," I assured him. "It's just that my brother will be here in five minutes. He's six feet four inches tall and a rugby halfback. He used to be a bouncer in a nightclub, and he's very protective toward me."

For a moment I thought it wouldn't work. For a moment I wondered if he'd heard it before—from Grizelda, because, after all, that's where I heard it. The imminent arrival of her brother was a ploy she used to extricate herself from a difficult situation, and she could afford to use it because she did have a brother with all these attributes. I mean, trust Grizelda. I'd never met him, but he often phoned her at the office.

It worked. Pierre left. "I will return," he said, "some other time." And I went to the kitchen and, true to my label of domesticity, cleaned out a cupboard and thought, *well, well.*

Emilio arrived a few evenings later. I was prospecting for supper in the fridge when the doorbell rang. Again I thought it might be John, and I tried to make a quick assessment. Would three eggs and a tin of sardines provide a banquet for two people? No, they would not, but never mind, a welcoming smile would do instead. So I opened the door and smiled brightly at Emilio. He was Italian, a chef, and he too was looking for Grizelda. "My fair Grizelda, where is she?"

I told him she had probably just left his hometown and offered him a cup of tea. Then I explained about supper. He took off his coat, hung it on a chair, and said, "I ama da cook. For you, my little one, I will create somethinga special."

Rolling up his sleeves, he created corned-beef fritters, which were out of this world, and crepes suzettes, using a couple of oranges and lemons left from a party. Afterward, we sat on the settee at a respectable distance, one at each end. His hand lay folded on his flat stomach, which would one day become ample. His head rested on the back of the settee in an attitude of repose. Half turning, he said softly, "Tell me, do you playa da ukulele?"

"No," I replied.

"Praisa da saints," he said, and fell asleep and snored gently through a TV play and the news. At eleven he stood up, kissed my hand and went home. I liked Emilio. He had the makings of a good husband.

London sweltered in a heat wave. The mornings were hushed and seemingly without movement. Tall office blocks shimmered in haze, and in the evening the westering sun blocked windows with sheets of flame. Trees wilted and children paddled in the pools around fountains.

I received another card from Grizelda.

From somewhere high above plains, in India, I think, with lush foliage and snowcapped mountains supporting a vivid blue sky. She said she couldn't wait to get home and put her feet up on the old settee. Great-aunt Grizelda was proving rather troublesome. Apparently she kept falling in love. First with a steward and then with a retired colonel.

"It's a good job," she wrote, "that I am here to keep an eye on her boyfriends."

And a good job, I thought, stacking the card with others behind the clock, *I am here to keep an eye on yours.*

After Emilio came Nevill, who fixed a kitchen shelf, and after Nevill, someone called Harry, who said he couldn't stay for a cup of tea but just wanted to return a pair of gloves Grizelda had left in his car. The only person I didn't have a chance to keep an eye on was John. He didn't arrive, and when there seemed no point in spending further hopeful evenings at home I went to visit Aunt Mildred.

She'd be wanting a visitor, I knew, just as I knew how her room would look. Nothing changed at Aunt Mildred's. She would be sitting by the fireplace, empty in this heat except for a log and a vase of daisies, contentedly knitting while she listened to the radio. No gallivanting around the world for Aunt Mildred. There would be cards from Grizelda on the mantelpiece, a lace cloth over a table, another vase of garden flowers placed on the windowsill beyond the neat curtain so that they could be enjoyed by others.

It was one of those still evenings that comes after a hot day when everything seems to be waiting. A bird immobile on a bough, waiting for its song. A petal about to fall. A flower in the border of the front garden, half opened, needing another dawn to complete the task.

The click of the gate was a sharp, clear noise in the silence. And then, from the neat terraced house came another noise. The notes of a ukulele obviously played by an expert. The music trilled and danced along the path in greeting and lent rhythm to my footsteps. The door opened automatically as I approached, and I went inside and there was John sitting on a chair in Aunt Mildred's tiny hall, cradling a ukulele in his arms.

We stared at each other. He smiled a slow, gentle smile. "You, too," I said, looking at the ukulele.

He nodded. "It runs in the family. Who do you think taught Grizelda?" He continued playing.

I didn't know the tune, but the notes were lively and captivating. And as I listened and watched his face, I suddenly realized—of course, the shape of the nose, the set of the head, the fair hair. Like Grizelda's....

"You're not..." I began. Surely this gentle man couldn't be Grizelda's brother. "You can't be—"

"Yes?" He put aside the ukulele.

"The rugby halfback who is very possessive about his womenfolk," I finished quickly.

"Right," he agreed. "On both counts."

"Who used to be a bouncer in a nightclub?"

He nodded again. "When I was at university, yes. Anything to earn an honest bob." He came over to me and touched my face. "I was waiting for you." His fingers traced my chin, touched my cheek. "I didn't know your address because I didn't know Grizelda's new address, but Aunt Mildred told me you visited every Friday and I knew if I waited here, you would come. I'm glad I've found you. Tell me, do you think you'd ever grow fond of the ukulele?"

"Oh yes," I said, knowing I would—if I am any judge of a gentle, committed touch, of instant love between two people—before the evening ended, long before Grizelda returned, very fond indeed. And with John, I might even learn to dance with bare "feets" in the park, on a tropical night, in London.

Just leave it to me.

9 FATHERS' RACE
BY GEMMA LEIGHTON

On the way to the sports ground, Susan Wells met Mrs. Sugden, whom she did not like.

"And tell me," said Mrs. Sugden as they walked, each with a daughter neatly in place at her side, "is that new husband of yours coming along today?"

Susan heard Jenny sigh, and she said quickly, "Yes, he is, Mrs. Sugden—at least I think so. If he can get away."

"That's nice."

"Yes," said Susan. "We think so."

Then they turned into the playing field from the hot pavement, and for a moment Susan was unable to say another word. The sun shone so blindingly that all the colors stood out with fierce strength: the acid-green grass, the moving white of the blouses and shirts as children ran here and there, the crisp yellow school flag that hung still and limp from the pavilion roof.

Susan loved moments like this—bright starts, fine

shows.... If only she and Jenny could be alone they could talk about it in their usual way, admiring things for each other...if only Mrs. Sugden would bustle off and take her silent Miriam with her.

"And is he going in for the fathers' race?" asked Mrs. Sugden.

"I'm sorry?"

"Your new husband—is he going in for the fathers' race?"

Susan felt her daughter's eyes turn quickly toward her, but she refused to meet that curious gaze. "Oh, no, I don't think so."

"No...?" said Mrs. Sugden.

There was something predetermined in that single word, something understanding that made Susan... was it angry? Perhaps—she hated herself for this—she was merely embarrassed. George on a running track.... No, she couldn't see it.

"He's coming straight from work.... He works most Saturdays, you see. He wouldn't have any kit or anything." Susan's excuses fell like accusations under Mrs. Sugden's charitable smile.

"Oh yes, it's so hot to run in ordinary clothes," said the woman, nodding as she spoke. "Are you running, Jenny?"

Susan's daughter looked sharply at Mrs. Sugden, then smiled and said, "In the hundred meters and the relay. Is Miriam?"

"No, dear," said Mrs. Sugden. "You know Miriam has a chest."

"Oh yes. Sorry."

Then Susan said, "Look, there's Jill. Do excuse us, Mrs. Sugden, we must just—"

There was a smile, a flutter of hands, and at last

they were free of her, walking toward the pavilion as Jenny whispered, "Silly thing."

"Jenny!"

"Well, she is—'That new husband.'" Jenny's brown eyes glimmered with rage. "She makes poor George sound like a fresh pair of socks."

"Can't you—"

"What, mommy?"

Susan stopped and looked almost sadly at her daughter, taking in the small, serious face, the straight hair touching her shoulders. How alike they were, she thought. How close in all things.

"Couldn't you call him daddy?" she asked at last. "Just occasionally? He would like it."

Jenny looked toward the pavilion where the teams were mustering, where teachers played official roles with bright silver whistles, which they blew and blew.

"Yes," said Jenny at last. "Eventually. But he's not my daddy like you're my mommy, is he?"

And for the second time that afternoon, Susan suffered guilt, because in her heart, the very center of her heart, she was glad to hear that special pledge of a special love.

Then a teacher with a whistle called out, "Jenny! Have you a number for the hundred?"

Jenny smiled an excuse at her mother, turned, and ran toward the pavilion with flashing steps. She was sure to win the hundred, thought Susan.

Susan and George Wells had been married for just two months, but still the less tactful of their acquaintances, like Mrs. Sugden, spoke of the "new husband" like some achievement to raise congratulatory eyebrows over.

It was as if they were saying, "Well done, Susan. Now you've got him—now you're all right."

Susan, following one of the senior boys to an empty deck chair, settled into it with a vague discomfort as—with customary thoroughness and care—she examined her own guilts and worries once more.

If only these people knew, she thought; if only they realized that getting a husband wasn't an end, wasn't something to be put in the bank to crow over. There were still so many problems, so much to be done....

The point, the whole point, about George's arrival in her life, was that he had come just as she'd felt that—at last—all her efforts to climb back from the misery of Peter's sudden illness and death had been rewarded. She and Jenny had done it together; they had become self-sufficient, had become, truthfully, happy once more.

And then George, new in their little Sussex village, had stood beside her at the squash-club bar saying, "I'm getting too old for this game...." And Susan had laughed at his rueful eyes.

The village had gossiped, friends had watched, weeks had passed. One day she introduced him to Jenny, who was painfully polite, but said later, "He's older than daddy...." And Susan had defended him so well that soon her daughter guessed: mommy was falling in love.

The child accepted what was happening with a careful grace that gradually became a kind of warmth. George made her smile; sometimes he made her laugh; sometimes she let him hold her hand on walks, sometimes she told him secrets. Sometimes.

"Call him daddy," Susan had said, because he had asked her, because he wanted it very much. And mother and child had stared at each other and each had wondered. . . .

Yes, Susan told herself, there was much to be done still, many pieces left to fit into the mosaic of this new life they were building.

"Mommy!"

The sharp cry brought the world back to Susan's eyes, and she smiled as she watched Jenny run up, trim in the white of her running clothes.

"Ready?" said Jenny. "I'm on in five minutes. Come on!"

Laughing now, Susan struggled out of the chair and stood up—just as she caught sight of George's tall, rather stooping figure at the entrance to the field. He was looking tentative, as always, staring about with shy uncertainty at the running children.

"Oh, there's your...there's George," said Susan. Why did she feel such a coward, such a traitor?

Jenny turned, saw him and shouted, "George! George!"

Other children stared at this piece of temerity. Teachers frowned, but said nothing. Susan recognized the confusion of pride and closeness and distance that lay behind the shout.

George identified them, waved and began striding in their direction, looking just a little out of place in his dark city suit. Other—younger—fathers wore jeans.

Mrs. Sugden got him within fifteen yards. Susan watched the approach and the swoop with an anxiety bordering on anger. Why couldn't they just mind their own business, she thought. Why couldn't she and George be left to build in peace?

"I was just telling your husband," said Mrs. Sugden

as they arrived, little Miriam still sadly in tow, "that your daughter has quite a reputation for running. One of the teachers was just telling me."

Odd how the words "your daughter" seemed to push Jenny to her mother alone, seemed to exclude poor George, who looked only hot and worried.

"You'll give our daughter a big head," said Susan, this time passing her own test.

"Now, I'm sure not!"

Laughter gaily rippled up and down some scale of amusement.

"Well, I'm dying to see her run," said George, kissing Susan—a fact observed—and turning to Jenny with a smile. "What is it, Jenny? Egg-and-spoon marathon? Underwater sack race?"

"Oh...George!" said the child, laughing.

"She *is* very good," Susan heard herself say.

There was a silence. Then Jenny said, "Come on, you two—cheer me on."

Jenny grabbed her mother's hand and began pulling her toward the track.

"Do excuse us again." Susan smiled at Mrs. Sugden.

George followed mother and daughter up the bright field, a dark figure among greens and blues and brilliant whites.

"On your marks...."

Runners poised like pictures on a page.

"Get set.... Go!"

The girls leaped from the line, and the cheers broke the tension with a snap. The figures streaked away over the grass between chalk lines.

"Come on, Jenny!" Susan and George shouted almost as one. "Come on!"

She won by yards. The cheers became loud talk as

Jenny trotted back to them looking immensely proud and bright.

"Well done!" George said at once. "Beautifully done!"

"Thanks. I didn't really think.... You know...."

Now, suddenly, the child seemed shy in front of him. Susan felt an odd, tender pain.

"Don't get cold, darling," she warned her daughter.

Later, as she and her husband strolled alone together by the edge of the wide, flat field, Susan tried to be especially nice to him, but because she was an honest person she felt awkward being so calculating, and the conversation sounded stilted.

At last, when they were well clear of the crowd, she stopped him and said, "George—you are happy with us, aren't you?"

"What?" His thin, distinguished face registered shock; the kind, tired eyes held hers as if in disbelief.

Susan struggled for words. "I mean, look...I don't know if you can understand, but this...you and me and Jenny...well, it's all still very new to me and I make mistakes. I mean, I'm trying to make it work properly, but sometimes...."

She waved a hand to indicate the things George might never have sensed: the ambivalent congratulations, the unadmitted fear of aging, the jealousy of a daughter's love....

"Only you're doing so well," she finished unhappily. "You're not making any mistakes at all."

What had she been trying to say?

George smiled the quiet, boyish smile she remembered from their first meeting, took Susan's hand and said, "I'm making mistakes every day, darling—only you're too kind to recognize them." She started to interrupt, but he held up a hand and went on. "And if you ask me, you may be trying just a little too hard. Honestly, love. Staring at the roots of a plant all the time.... There's got to be time for growth."

They looked at each other in silence for a moment. A whistle blew somewhere, hard and shrill. Susan stirred like a child and said, almost vacantly, "She's running again soon."

They turned and began walking back toward the track.

"Sometimes," George repeated quietly as they walked, "it really is best just to leave things."

A loudspeaker at the pavilion bellowed, "And just a reminder that at the end of the day there will be a fathers' race for all you dads with a bit of energy...."

George and Susan walked on in silence.

Jenny ran the final leg of the relay and came first, to roaring cheers. When she had recovered, they bought tea and sat on the grass watching the boys at the high jump. George still looked hot in his suit, but he resisted when Susan suggested, tactfully, that he remove the jacket.

"Are you going to run, George?" asked Jenny suddenly.

"But I haven't anything to wear. I didn't think...."

"Oh, don't go on at him," said Susan. "It's far too hot today. You heard what I told—" she hesitated, caught his eye, and finished "—Mrs. Sugden."

George smiled, but said nothing at all. There was the smallest pause, and then Jenny sighed and said, "Oh, go on, George. All the other girls have got people in."

"All right," he said suddenly. "I will."

"What?" Susan couldn't help herself. George, against all those young fathers?

George looked straight at her and said, "I'll run."

"Oh, good!" Jenny grinned her pleasure, but the two adults stared at each other in silence for a moment longer.

Susan said almost dismissively, "It's a long way. Four hundred meters, someone said. You can't do that, can you?"

"Ah, I think so."

But George said no more, and Jenny, as if sensing a problem, took the smile from her face and sipped tea.

The afternoon passed. The boys on the high jump set a new school record; there were small certificates for all winners, including two for Jenny. George clapped louder and longer than anyone—it was almost embarrassing.

Then the headmaster said, "And now for the most awful event...." He was a young man and he liked jokes. "The fathers' race!"

There were a few cheers. Someone clapped. Then nothing happened until, at last, one or two of the men began sidling into the pavilion to change.

"George? What are you going to run in?" Jenny was frowning as she stood at her stepfather's side.

George ducked his head in mock embarrassment and held up his arms. "This," he said. "It's all I've got. I did tell you."

"Oh."

Susan could see her daughter's embarrassment. She wondered whether George could.

"A lot of other fathers won't have proper kit, dear," she said.

But, as it turned out, George was the only one without the right clothes. The other fathers—a dozen or so of them—arrived at the starting line on the edge of the field in a mixture of track suits, bright shirts and running shoes...much of it left over from college perhaps, but still serviceable. George took off his jacket and socks and shoes and went to stand with them in an uneasy fashion. Susan felt inexpressibly sad, but did not know for whom. Jenny was silent.

The large crowd chattered and laughed; the event had a tension about it that they all felt. These were mostly young men at the line, and their faces were serious.

"On your marks...." The headmaster's voice silenced all talk.

"Get set...."

"Go!"

The crowd shouted, the runners set off, the race began.

To cover four hundred meters, the fathers had to run once around the field, and by the time they had covered the first fifty paces a pattern was emerging.

A fit-looking young man with blond hair and a red shirt was easily in the lead, then came three more fathers, then a gap, then George looking silly in his flapping shirt and trousers, then the rest of the bunch.

The children were shouting and screaming, the howls of "Daddy...daddy..." rolling over and over the field, reaching a crescendo as the runners attacked the second hundred meters.

"Come on, George!" shouted Susan. "Come on, George!"

Jenny was still silent. The crowd about them

roared. The runners moved on, and by now—strangely—George was lying third. How odd, thought Susan, when he was so poor at squash....

His face looked strained and tight; his eyes were on the man in front.

Throughout the next part of the race, the blond man made further efforts to increase his lead, egged on by screams and shouts.

George overtook the second man, and Susan saw Jenny flutter and then become calm and silent once more. George's face shone red across the field. He could never last the pace, she thought, could never manage.

As the runners spurted yet again, the children screamed, "Come on! Daddy! Daddy!"

Susan shouted, "George!"

Jenny said nothing, though she watched—saw the red face, the straining limbs.

A hundred and fifty meters to go. The fathers at the back were suffering, and some in the smartest track suits were dropping out with sheepish smiles.

At the front, the young blond man glanced back over his shoulder at George and increased his speed. "George!" shouted Susan. "Come on, George!"

As they approached the last hundred, George was twenty paces back and trying very hard—too hard, thought Susan suddenly, much too hard. It's only a race, she wanted to shout, just a silly race.

His face was contorted, his arms were pumping fiercely. His bare feet pounded the bright grass....

But he was gaining on the leader and the man knew it. As the two of them flashed around toward the final bend, the children were shrieking wildly, and Susan was jumping and shouting, too, despite her anxiety.

"George! George!"

Jenny, bright eyed, said nothing.

And little by little, George cut into the lead, thrusting himself with stiff, painful intensity nearer the man in front.

"George!" screamed Susan. "Come on, George!"

Then she glanced once at her daughter, hesitated, and in the space of a second understood many things. And she fell silent. Despite the excitement, the fear, the haunting hope of victory, Susan said nothing.

Above the roar of general encouragement, she could hear one girl shouting to the blond leader, "Daddy! Come on...daddy!"

Susan, not looking at Jenny now, still kept silent. She felt her daughter's eyes on her, but though she ached with excitement, she held her tongue.

George gained inch by painful inch.

Suddenly a new voice screamed, "Daddy!" Jenny's shout cut through Susan's heart like fire. "Daddy! Daddy! Daddy!"

The crowd's voice lifted and buried the single voice, but Susan heard it still. Heard it as the runners drew level, heard it as George seemed to falter at last, heard it as, with two paces to go, George's face said that this was, after all, too much for him....

George came in second by a couple of feet, and he lay down on the grass far from the crowd and buried his exhausted face in his arms.

Jenny was at his side at once, touching his drenched shirt, jabbering, "You nearly did it, daddy! You nearly got him! If you'd had proper shorts and things—are you listening, daddy? If maybe you'd gone a bit faster at the start...."

The child chattered on, unaware perhaps of

George's expression as he raised his face at last toward her, listening, examining.

Susan, standing back, began to hurry toward them to join in the excited family scene. Then Mrs. Sugden came up and said, "Well, what an exciting finish."

And something, not Mrs. Sugden, made Susan stop, made her turn and smile and not join her husband and daughter after all.

Talking to Mrs. Sugden, she saw George stand, saw Jenny take his hand in a perfectly natural gesture and lead him away toward the pavilion, still chattering. She saw George's face and, though she ached to go with them, to say something, to do something...she didn't. She stayed and talked to Mrs. Sugden, whom she did not like.

A piece of the mosaic had fitted into place.

George was right. Sometimes it was best to do nothing at all.

Lois knelt so that she was face-to-face with the puppy, through the none-too-clean shop window. Its eyes revealed the perpetual optimism of a canine, archetypal born loser.

My, but he was ugly. Apart from his eyes. Their dark velvet depths compensated for the squat little body and flat, thick head. His tail was pure cartoon, absurdly plumed, curling onto his back and wagging tentatively, warily, as though he knew how fleeting this blissful moment of communication was likely to be.

Lois looked hard at the unprepossessing little mongrel and wondered if her eyes expressed her personal despair so blatantly.

She doubted it. At the last check they had seemed perfectly familiar and normal. Wide and long lashed, the pale, smudgy eye shadow creating just the right highlights, her brows professionally shaped.

Someone had once said that eyes were the mirrors of the soul. Maybe she'd had too much practice recently, hiding the inner doubts, controlling the despair that wouldn't be banished.

She looked at the dog again. His eyes quite definitely reflected his soul. They were unmistakably saying that he wished her to claim him as her own.

Lois stood up and leaned one hand against the window to steady herself. And what would David say to that little maneuver?

Fifteen years ago, she'd have telephoned him and he'd have arranged to meet her. Together, they'd have shared and mulled over this tremendous decision. Would the flat be big enough, was it fair to have a puppy when they were both working? Their conclusion would have been born of mutual consideration, of total communication.

She closed her eyes briefly as the panic wave of depression swept through her, leaving her weak and trembling. The dog had lain down now, still watching her, but no longer hopeful.

Lois mouthed a foolish, self-conscious, "I'm so sorry" at him through the window and turned away quickly, not looking back.

Fifteen years was a long time ago and circumstances change. She didn't work now—and their town house was big enough to stable a racehorse, never mind a dog.

She could picture David's reaction as clearly as if he were with her now: "You want a puppy? You actually want to buy a dog, to burden yourself with all sorts of idiotic training and responsibilities? Now, when the children are settled at school and we've found our dream house...."

His reasoning was sound, to be fair. He'd worked long, hard hours to achieve his success and all that went with it. And Lois had gone along with the blueprint plan. Instead of daydreaming or doing the odd watercolor, she'd gone to Cordon Bleu classes and courses on flower arranging.

And gradually their life-style had settled on its new axis, with Simon and Fiona at expensive but congenial boarding schools, plus the acquisition of the new town house with its thick pile carpets and treasured, long-sought antiques. David's solid grind at the office was relieved by their early spring holiday in Majorca and regular winter skiing fortnight in Austria.

A far cry from their first home, an upstairs flat, with David cramming at night school after work and Lois herself coming home to cook and iron after a full day at university. A far cry indeed. A world of separation.

The words caught at Lois's heart. That was the whole root of the trouble. They were entering into a dangerously separate existence, with the children away, David a slave to the demands of business, and Lois herself flitting from coffee morning to golf club to bridge party.

And in all this the mystery was how could such full living produce such a dearth of conversation at the end of the day? Even in bed, their communication had become purely physical, almost without warmth.

Today at lunch at the plush department store, she had caught sight of herself and her three friends in the mirrored wall behind them. Four glossy, attractive women, playing their familiar conversation game—fashion, hairstyles, education, dishwashers, local gossip. Lois had sat back, deliberately detaching herself, and had wondered where their idealism had gone. They had all been young, hopeful and earnest. Didn't they need to dream anymore?

She couldn't bear another moment and had excused herself before the coffee arrived. She had said goodbye quickly, longing for fresh air, to be able to walk and walk, to allow her mind to clear itself, to assess, to attempt a solution.

And then she'd found herself in the narrow, dark side streets, and she'd seen the puppy. The thought of him now, sleeping in that grimy corner of the shop made her eyes fill with tears and in a sudden blaze of decision, she looked for a telephone kiosk.

David's secretary's impeccably trained voice pleasantly informed Lois that he was rather busy. Was it urgent? Lois said that indeed it was, and that she wished to speak to her husband now.

David's voice sounded strangely welcoming and showed not a vestige of impatience, and for a second, it threw Lois. But she went ahead with her campaign.

"A puppy? From some pet shop?" David queried, his tone controlled but with the surprise showing.

Lois was explicit. Yes, a puppy, and yes, it was a pet shop in a filthy back lane called Blackgate. And the puppy was just as unprepossessing. Black-and-white, with a ridiculous tail and it was more than probably flea ridden, but she wanted it.

David's patience was amazingly limitless. He went carefully through all the arguments. The inconvenience, the impracticalities—the oyster-colored carpets for one. She remained adamant and he changed his tack. Well, what about a poodle, or a Siamese cat from some reputable source? Why this particular dog?

Lois felt the tears running down her impeccably

colored cheeks. She didn't know where the words, the emotions, came from. Deep down, she supposed, rising like a phoenix from the ashes of her despair, which had built up over the years. She left nothing out. Not the children at school, not the town house, not the golf club, not David's presidential company tours of the globe, not even their cold marriage bed.

"What have we got now? Apart from oyster carpets and dishwashers and your fifty-three drip-dry shirts?" she shouted. "Think of what we used to have. The laughter, the tears, the peaks, the valleys. I want the children around me, I want you, David. I want to know what you think, what you feel, what you want. There was a time when we didn't need words. Now we can't even find them."

David said quietly, "You seem to be doing all right in that direction. Have you finished, or are there some more home truths to be spilled?"

Lois was totally exhausted and shivering uncontrollably, so the telephone shook in her hand. She felt suddenly alone. She said, "No, I've finished. And forget about the dog."

She left the kiosk and walked some more, then found a cinema showing an old American musical. She fell asleep after half an hour and awoke when the next film was beginning. She repaired her makeup, then drove home.

As she pulled into the drive she saw David's car. She sat for a moment, totally enervated, not wanting to move. How would he be, she wondered: furious, or unctuously understanding, proffering sherries and a meal out somewhere, or an extra holiday? Anything to allay the horrors of an incipient neurotic wife.

He'd already opened the front door and she saw

that he was angry. And not looking at all himself. Sort of disheveled, frantic and most curiously garbed.

"I could kill you," he said. And her heart flared in the wildest optimism because his face and his magnificent gray eyes were saying anything but that.

"Don't you ever dare do this to me again. I've been almost out of my mind. I've already rung around so many friends so many times, they obviously think you've run off with the milkman. The police were the next on my list."

Lois said wearily, "Why are you wearing that ridiculous apron? It's Mrs. Mason's jam-making apron."

David took her hand and led her upstairs. "You may well ask. I'm wearing it because the job I'm doing requires a large all-enveloping garment, and this was all I could think of."

He opened the door to the bathroom, their beautiful, opulent bathroom with the exquisite chestnut brown suite and the thick-piled oyster carpet. But the thick pile was strangely sodden and bedraggled, and in the midst of a pile of her newest, fluffiest, most expensive towels, sat an unprepossessing mongrel of familiar features and beautiful brown soulful eyes.

David said, "You were right about one thing. He is flea ridden. Extremely!"

He looked at her for a moment, and suddenly there was no laughter in his eyes. Lois read the fear, the nascent hope, the plea for a second chance. He said quietly, "You were right about a few things actually. And he's the beginning of things to come."

And then the laughter was back, and he threw her a towel. "Well, get working, woman. He was your idea."

And for the next few moments, the gold-plated,

Italian-tiled luxury of the bathroom was a chaotic muddle, with Lois in David's arms, being held against him, long and hard, while one very new canine addition to the household leaped madly about them, determined to be part of this glorious celebration.

Get this book FREE!

Mail to:

Harlequin Reader Service

In the U.S.
2504 West Southern Ave.
Tempe, AZ 85282

In Canada
P.O. Box 2800, Postal Station A
5170 Yonge St., Willowdale, Ont. M2N 5T5

YES! I want to be one of the first to discover **Harlequin American Romance.** Send me FREE and without obligation *Twice in a Lifetime.* If you do not hear from me after I have examined my FREE book, please send me the 4 new **Harlequin American Romances** each month as soon as they come off the presses. I understand that I will be billed only $2.25 for each book (total $9.00). There are no shipping or handling charges. There is no minimum number of books that I have to purchase. In fact, I may cancel this arrangement at any time. *Twice in a Lifetime* is mine to keep as a FREE gift, even if I do not buy any additional books.   154 BPA NAWG

Name _____ (please print)

Address _____ Apt. no.

City _____ State/Prov. _____ Zip/Postal Code

Signature (If under 18, parent or guardian must sign.)

AMR-SUB-2

Take these
4 best-selling novels
FREE

Yes! Four sophisticated, contemporary love stories by four world-famous authors of romance FREE, as your introduction to the Harlequin Presents subscription plan. Thrill to **Anne Mather**'s passionate story BORN OUT OF LOVE, set in the Caribbean.... Travel to darkest Africa in **Violet Winspear**'s TIME OF THE TEMPTRESS....Let **Charlotte Lamb** take you to the fascinating world of London's Fleet Street in MAN'S WORLD....Discover beautiful Greece in **Sally Wentworth**'s moving romance SAY HELLO TO YESTERDAY.

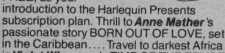

Harlequin Presents...   *The very finest in romance fiction*

Join the millions of avid Harlequin readers all over the world who delight in the magic of a really exciting novel. EIGHT great NEW titles published EACH MONTH! Each month you will get to know exciting, interesting, true-to-life people .... You'll be swept to distant lands you've dreamed of visiting. .... Intrigue, adventure, romance, and the destiny of many lives will thrill you through each Harlequin Presents novel.

Get all the latest books before they're sold out!

As a Harlequin subscriber you actually receive your personal copies of the latest Presents novels immediately after they come off the press, so you're sure of getting all 8 each month.

Cancel your subscription whenever you wish!

You don't have to buy any minimum number of books. Whenever you decide to stop your subscription just let us know and we'll cancel all further shipments.